Count Lev Nikolayevich Tolstoy (9 September [O.S. 28 August] 1828 – 20 November [O.S. 7 November] 1910), usually referred to in English as Leo Tolstoy, was a Russian writer who is regarded as one of the greatest authors of all time. He received multiple nominations for Nobel Prize in Literature every year from 1902 to 1906, and nominations for Nobel Peace Prize in 1901, 1902 and 1910, and his miss of the prize is a major Nobel prize controversy. Born to an aristocratic Russian family in 1828, he is best known for the novels War and Peace (1869) and Anna Karenina (1877), often cited as pinnacles of realist fiction. He first achieved literary acclaim in his twenties with his semi-autobiographical trilogy, Childhood, Boyhood, and Youth (1852–1856), and Sevastopol Sketches (1855), based upon his experiences in the Crimean War. Tolstoy's fiction includes dozens of short stories and several novellas such as The Death of Ivan Ilyich (1886), Family Happiness (1859), and Hadji Murad (1912). He also wrote plays and numerous philosophical essays. (Source: Wikipedia)

Literary works:

The Autobiographical Trilogy
Childhood (1852)
Boyhood (1854)
Youth (1856)
War and Peace (1869)
Anna Karenina (1877)
Resurrection (1899)
Family Happiness (1859)
The Cossacks (1863)
The Death of Ivan Ilyich (1886)
The Kreutzer Sonata (1889)
The Devil (1911)
The Forged Coupon (1911)
Hadji Murat (1917)

THRONE CLASSICS

THREE DAYS IN THE VILLAGE

AND OTHER SKETCHES

LEO TOLSTOY

This is a work of fiction. Names, characters, places, and incidents either are the product of the author's imagination or are used fictitiously. Any resemblance to actual persons, living or dead, events, or locales is entirely coincidental.

First Printing: 2019

ISBN 978-93-89438-89-5 (paperback)

ISBN 978-93-89438-90-1 (Hardcover)

ISBN 978-93-89438-91-8 (eBook)

Published by Throne Classics

www.throneclassics.com

Contents

THREE DAYS IN THE VILLAGE

AND OTHER SKETCHES

THREE DAYS IN THE VILLAGE

FIRST DAY-TRAMPS

Something entirely new, unseen and unheard-of formerly, has lately shown itself in our country districts. To our village, consisting of eighty homesteads, from half a dozen to a dozen cold, hungry, tattered tramps come every day, wanting a night's lodging.

These people, ragged, half-naked, barefoot, often ill, and extremely dirty, come into the village and go to the village policeman. That they should not die in the street of hunger and exposure, he quarters them on the inhabitants of the village, regarding only the peasants as "inhabitants." He does not take them to the squire, who besides his own ten rooms has ten other apartments: office, coachman's room, laundry, servants' and upper-servants' hall and so on; nor does he take them to the priest or deacon or shopkeeper, in whose houses, though not large, there is still some spare room; but he takes them to the peasants, whose whole family, wife, daughters-in-law, unmarried daughters, and big and little children, all live in one room—sixteen, nineteen, or twenty-three feet long. And the master of the hut takes the cold, hungry, stinking, ragged, dirty man, and not merely gives him a night's lodging, but feeds him as well.

"When you sit down to table yourself," an old peasant householder told me, "it's impossible not to invite him too, or your own soul accepts nothing. So one feeds him and gives him a drink of tea."

Those are the nightly visitors. But during the day, not two or three, but ten or more such visitors call at each hut, and again it is: "Why, it is impossible...," etc.

And for almost every tramp the housewife cuts a slice of bread, thinner or thicker according to the man's appearance—though she knows her rye will not last till next harvest.

"If you were to give to all who come, a loaf [the big peasant loaf of black bread] would not last a day," some housewives said to me. "So sometimes one hardens one's heart and refuses!"

And this goes on every day, all over Russia. An enormous yearly-increasing army of beggars, cripples, administrative exiles, helpless old men, and above all unemployed workmen, lives—that is to say, shelters itself from cold and wet—and is actually fed by the hardest-worked and poorest class, the country peasants.

We have Workhouses,[1] Foundlings' Hospitals, Boards of Public Relief, and all sorts of philanthropic organisations in our towns; and in all those institutions, in buildings with electric light, parquet floors, neat servants, and various well-paid attendants, thousands of helpless people of all sorts are sheltered. But however many such there may be, they are but a drop in the ocean of the enormous (unnumbered, but certainly enormous) population which now tramps destitute over Russia, and is sheltered and fed apart from any institutions, solely by the village peasants whose own Christian feelings induce them to bear this heavy and gigantic tax.

Just think what people who are not peasants would say, if—even once a week—such a shivering, starving, dirty, lousy tramp were placed in each of their bedrooms! But the peasants not only house them, but feed them and give them tea, because "one's own soul accepts nothing unless one has them to table."

In the more remote parts of Sarátof, Tambóf, and other Provinces, the peasants do not wait for the policeman to bring these tramps, but always receive them and feed them of their own accord.

And, as is the case with all really good deeds, the peasants do this without knowing that they are doing a good deed; and yet it is not merely a good deed "for one's soul," but is of enormous importance for the whole of Russian society. It is of such importance for Russian society because, but for this peasant population and the Christian feeling that lives so strongly in it, it is difficult to imagine what the fate would be, not only of these hundreds of thousands of unfortunate, houseless tramps, but of all the well-to-do—and especially of the wealthy who have their houses in the country.

It is only necessary to see the state of privation and suffering to which these homeless tramps have come or have been brought, and to imagine the mental condition they must be in, and to realise that it is only this help rendered to them by the peasants that restrains them from committing violence, which would be quite natural in their position, upon those who possess in superfluity all the things these unfortunates lack to keep themselves alive.

So that it is not the philanthropic organisations, not the Government with its police and all its juridical institutions, that protects us, the well-to-do, from being attacked by those who wander, cold, hungry, and homeless, after having sunk—or, for the most part, having been brought—to the lowest depths of poverty and despair; but we are protected, as well as fed and supported, by that same basic strength of the Russian nation—the peasantry.

Yes! Were it not that there is among Russia's vast peasant population a deep religious consciousness of the brotherhood of all men, not only would these homeless people, having reached the last stages of despair, have long since destroyed the houses of the rich, in spite of any police force (there are and must be so few of them in country districts), but they would even have killed all who stood in their way. So that we ought not to be horrified or surprised when we hear or read of people being robbed, or killed that they may be robbed, but we should understand and remember that if such things happen as seldom as they do, we owe this to the unselfish help rendered by the peasants to this unfortunate tramping population.

Every day from ten to fifteen people come to our house to beg. Some among them are regular beggars, who for some reason have chosen that means of livelihood, and having clothed and shod themselves as best they might, and having made sacks to hold what they collect, have started out to tramp the country. Among them some are blind, and some have lost a leg or an arm; and sometimes, though rarely, there are women and children among them.

But these are only a small part. The majority of the beggars that come now are passers-by, without a beggar's sack, mostly young, and not crippled. They are all in a most pitiable state, barefoot, half-naked, emaciated, and shivering with cold. You ask them, "Where are you going?" The answer is always the same: "To look for work"; or, "Have been looking for work, but found none, and am making my way home. There's no work; they are shutting down everywhere." Many of these people are returning from exile.

A few days ago I was barely awake when our servant, Ilyá Vasílyevitch, told me:

"There are five tramps waiting near the porch."

"Take some money there is on the table, and give it them," said I.

Ilyá Vasílyevitch took it, and, as is the custom, gave each of them five copecks [five farthings]. About an hour passed. I went out into the porch. A dreadfully tattered little man with a sickly face, swollen eyelids, restless eyes, and boots all falling to pieces, began bowing, and held out a certificate to me.

"Have you received something?"

"Your Excellency, what am I to do with five copecks?... Your Excellency, put yourself in my place! Please, your Excellency, look ... please see!" and he shows me his clothing. "Where am I to go to, your Excellency?" (it is "Excellency" after every word, though his face expresses hatred). "What am I to do? Where am I to go?"

I tell him that I give to all alike. He continues to entreat, and demands that I should read his certificate. I refuse. He kneels down. I ask him to leave me.

"Very well! That means, it seems, that I must put an end to myself! That's all that's left me to do.... Give me something, if only a trifle!"

I give him twenty copecks, and he goes away, evidently angry.

There are a great many such peculiarly insistent beggars, who feel they have a right to demand their share from the rich. They are literate for the most part, and some of them are even well-read persons on whom the Revolution has had an effect. These men, unlike the ordinary, old-fashioned beggars, look on the rich, not as on people who wish to save their souls by distributing alms, but as on highwaymen and robbers who suck the blood of the working classes. It often happens that a beggar of this sort does no work himself and carefully avoids work, and yet considers himself, in the name of the workers, not merely justified, but bound, to hate the robbers of the people—that is to say, the rich—and to hate them from the depths of his heart; and if, instead of demanding from them, he begs, that is only a pretence.

There are a great number of these men, many of them drunkards, of whom one feels inclined to say, "It's their own fault"; but there are also a great many tramps of quite a different type: meek, humble, and very pathetic, and it is terrible to think of their position.

Here is a tall, good-looking man, with nothing on over his short, tattered jacket. His boots are bad and trodden down. He has a good, intelligent face. He takes off his cap and begs in the ordinary way. I give him something, and he thanks me. I ask him where he comes from and where he is going to.

"From Petersburg, home to our village in Toúla Government."

I ask him, "Why on foot?"

"It's a long story," he answers, shrugging his shoulders.

I ask him to tell it me. He relates it with evident truthfulness.

"I had a good place in an office in Petersburg, and received thirty roubles [three guineas] a month. Lived very comfortably. I have read your books War and Peace and Anna Karénina," says he, again smiling a particularly pleasant smile. "Then my folks at home got the idea of migrating to Siberia, to the Province of Tomsk." They wrote to him asking whether he would agree to sell his share of land in the old place. He agreed. His people left, but the land allotted them in Siberia turned out worthless. They spent all they had, and came back. Being now landless, they are living in hired lodgings in their former village, and work for wages. It happened, just at the same time, that he lost his place in Petersburg. It was not his doing. The firm he was with became bankrupt, and dismissed its employees. "And just then, to tell the truth, I came across a seamstress." He smiled again. "She quite entangled me.... I used to help my people, and now see what a smart chap I have become!... Ah well, God is not without mercy; maybe I'll manage somehow!"

He was evidently an intelligent, strong, active fellow, and only a series of misfortunes had brought him to his present condition.

Take another: his legs swathed in strips of rag; girdled with a rope; his clothing quite threadbare and full of small holes, evidently not torn, but worn-out to the last degree; his face, with its high cheek-bones, pleasant, intelligent, and sober. I give him the customary five copecks, and he thanks me and we start a conversation. He has been an administrative exile in Vyátka. It was bad enough there, but it is worse here. He is going to Ryazán, where he used to live. I ask him what he has been. "A newspaper man. I took the papers round."

"For what were you exiled?"

"For selling forbidden literature."

We began talking about the Revolution. I told him my opinion, that the evil was all in ourselves; and that such an enormous power as that of the Government cannot be destroyed by force. "Evil outside ourselves will only be destroyed when we have destroyed it within us," said I.

"That is so, but not for a long time."

"It depends on us."

"I have read your book on Revolution."

"It is not mine, but I agree with it."

"I wished to ask you for some of your books."

"I should be very pleased.... Only I'm afraid they may get you into trouble. I'll give you the most harmless."

"Oh, I don't care! I am no longer afraid of anything.... Prison is better for me than this! I am not afraid of prison.... I even long for it sometimes," he said sadly.

"What a pity it is that so much strength is wasted uselessly!" said I. "How people like you destroy your own lives!... Well, and what do you mean to do now?"

"I?" he said, looking intently into my face.

At first, while we talked about past events and general topics, he had answered me boldly and cheerfully; but as soon as our conversation referred to himself personally and he noticed my sympathy, he turned away, hid his eyes with his sleeve, and I noticed that the back of his head was shaking.

And how many such people there are!

They are pitiable and pathetic, and they, too, stand on the threshold beyond which a state of despair begins that makes even a kindly man ready to go all lengths.

"Stable as our civilisation may seem to us," says Henry George, "disintegrating forces are already developing within it. Not in deserts and forests, but in city slums and on the highways, the barbarians are being bred who will do for our civilisation what the Huns and Vandals did for the civilisation of former ages."

Yes! What Henry George foretold some twenty years ago, is happening now before our eyes, and in Russia most glaringly—thanks to the amazing blindness of our Government, which carefully undermines the foundations on which alone any and every social order stands or can stand.

We have the Vandals foretold by Henry George quite ready among us in Russia. And, strange as it may seem to say so, these Vandals, these doomed men, are specially dreadful here among our deeply religious population. These Vandals are specially dreadful here, because we have not the restraining principles of convention, propriety, and public opinion, that are so strongly developed among the European nations. We have either real, deep, religious feeling, or—as in Sténka Rázin and Pougatchéf—a total absence of any restraining principle: and, dreadful to say, this army of Sténkas and Pougatchéfs is growing greater and greater, thanks to the Pougatchéf-like conduct of our Government in these later days, with its horrors of police violence, insane banishments, imprisonments, exiles, fortresses, and daily executions.

Such actions release the Sténka Rázins from the last remnants of moral restraint. "If the learned gentlefolk act like that, God Himself permits us to do so," say and think they.

I often receive letters from that class of men, chiefly exiles. They know I have written something about not resisting evil by violence, and for the greater part they retort ungrammatically, though with great fervour, that what the Government and the rich are doing to the poor, can and must be answered only in one way: "Revenge, revenge, revenge!"

Yes! The blindness of our Government is amazing. It does not and will not see that all it does to disarm its enemies merely increases their number and energy. Yes! These people are terrible, terrible for the Government and for the rich, and for those who live among the rich.

But besides the feeling of terror these people inspire, there is also another feeling, much more imperative than that of fear, and one we cannot help experiencing towards those who, by a series of accidents, have fallen into this terrible condition of vagrancy. That feeling is one of shame and sympathy.

And it is not fear, so much as shame and pity, that should oblige us, who are not in that condition, to respond in one way or other to this new and terrible phenomenon in Russian life.[2]

SECOND DAY-THE LIVING AND THE DYING

As I sat at my work, Ilyá Vasílyevitch entered softly and, evidently reluctant to disturb me at my work, told me that some wayfarers and a woman had been waiting a long time to see me.

"Here," I said, "please take this, and give it them."

"The woman has come about some business."

I told him to ask her to wait a while, and continued my work. By the time I came out, I had quite forgotten about her, till I saw a young peasant woman with a long, thin face, and clad very poorly and too lightly for the weather, appear from behind a corner of the house.

"What do you want? What is the matter?"

"I've come to see you, your Honour."

"Yes ... what about? What is the matter?"

"To see you, your Honour."

"Well, what is it?"

"He's been taken wrongfully.... I'm left with three children."

"Who's been taken, and where to?"

"My husband ... sent off to Krapívny."

"Why? What for?"

"For a soldier, you know. But it's wrong—because, you see, he's the breadwinner! We can't get on without him.... Be a father to us, sir!"

"But how is it? Is he the only man in the family?"

"Just so ... the only man!"

"Then how is it they have taken him, if he's the only man?"

"Who can tell why they've done it?... Here am I, left alone with the children! There's nothing for me but to die.... Only I'm sorry for the children! My last hope is in your kindness, because, you see, it was not right!"

I wrote down the name of her village, and her name and surname, and told her I would see about it and let her know.

"Help me, if it's only ever so little!... The children are hungry, and, God's my witness, I haven't so much as a crust. The baby is worst of all ... there's no milk in my breasts. If only the Lord would take him!"

"Haven't you a cow?" I asked.

"A cow? Oh, no!... Why, we're all starving!" said she, crying, and trembling all over in her tattered coat.

I let her go, and prepared for my customary walk. It turned out that the doctor, who lives with us, was going to visit a patient in the village the soldier's wife had come from, and another patient in the village where the District Police Station is situated, so I joined him, and we drove off together.

I went into the Police Station, while the doctor attended to his business in that village.

The District Elder was not in, nor the clerk, but only the clerk's assistant—a clever lad whom I knew. I asked him about the woman's husband, and why, being the only man in the family, he had been taken as a conscript.

The clerk's assistant looked up the particulars, and replied that the woman's husband was not the only man in the family: he had a brother.

"Then why did she say he was the only one?"

"She lied! They always do," replied he, with a smile.

I made some inquiries about other matters I had to attend to, and then the doctor returned from visiting his patient, and we drove towards the village in which the soldier's wife lived. But before we were out of the first village, a girl of about twelve came quickly across the road towards us.

"I suppose you're wanted?" I said to the doctor.

"No, it's your Honour I want," said the girl to me.

"What is it?"

"I've come to your Honour, as mother is dead, and we are left orphans—five of us. Help us!... Think of our needs!"

"Where do you come from?"

The girl pointed to a brick house, not badly built.

"From here ... that is our house. Come and see for yourself!"

I got out of the sledge, and went towards the house. A woman came out and asked me in. She was the orphans' aunt. I entered a large, clean room; all the children were there, four of them: besides the eldest girl—two boys, a girl, and another boy of about two. Their aunt told me all about the family's circumstances. Two years ago the father had been killed in a mine. The widow tried to get compensation, but failed. She was left with four children; the fifth was born after her husband's death. She struggled on alone as best she could, hiring a labourer at first to work her land. But without her husband things went worse and worse. First they had to sell their cow, then the horse, and at last only two sheep were left. Still they managed to live somehow; but two months ago the woman herself fell ill and died, leaving five children, the eldest twelve years old.

"They must get along as best they can. I try to help them, but can't do much. I can't think what's to become of them! I wish they'd die!... If one could only get them into some Orphanage—or at least some of them!"

The eldest girl evidently understood and took in the whole of my conversation with her aunt.

"If at least one could get little Nicky placed somewhere! It's awful; one can't leave him for a moment," said she, pointing to the sturdy little two-year old urchin, who with his little sister was merrily laughing at something or other, and evidently did not at all share his aunt's wish.

I promised to take steps to get one or more of the children into an

Orphanage. The eldest girl thanked me, and asked when she should come for an answer. The eyes of all the children, even of Nicky, were fixed on me, as on some fairy being capable of doing anything for them.

Before I had reached the sledge, after leaving the house, I met an old man. He bowed, and at once began speaking about these same orphans.

"What misery!" he said; "it's pitiful to see them. And the eldest little girlie, how she looks after them—just like a mother! Wonderful how the Lord helps her! It's a mercy the neighbours don't forsake them, or they'd simply die of hunger, the dear little things!... They are the sort of people it does no harm to help," he added, evidently advising me to do so.

I took leave of the old man, the aunt, and the little girl, and drove with the doctor to the woman who had been to see me that morning.

At the first house we came to, I inquired where she lived. It happened to be the house of a widow I know very well; she lives on the alms she begs, and she has a particularly importunate and pertinacious way of extorting them. As usual, she at once began to beg. She said she was just now in special need of help to enable her to rear a calf.

"She's eating me and the old woman out of house and home. Come in and see her."

"And how is the old woman?"

"What about the old woman?... She's hanging on...."

I promised to come and see, not so much the calf as the old woman, and again inquired where the soldier's wife lived. The widow pointed to the next hut but one, and hastened to add that no doubt they were poor, but her brother-in-law "does drink dreadfully!"

Following her instructions, I went to the next house but one.

Miserable as are the huts of all the poor in our villages, it is long since I saw one so dilapidated as that. Not only the whole roof, but the walls were so crooked that the windows were aslant.

Inside, it was no better than outside. The brick oven took up one-third of the black, dirty little hut, which to my surprise was full of people. I thought I should find the widow alone with her children; but here was a sister-in-law (a young woman with children) and an old mother-in-law. The soldier's wife herself had just returned from her visit to me, and was warming herself on the top of the oven. While she was getting down, her mother-in-law began telling me of their life. Her two sons had lived together at first, and they all managed to feed themselves.

"But who remain together nowadays? All separate," the garrulous old woman went on. "The wives began quarrelling, so the brothers separated, and life became still harder. We had little land, and only managed to live by their wage-labour; and now they have taken Peter as a soldier! So where is she to turn to with her children? She's living with us now, but we can't manage to feed them all! We can't think what we are to do. They say he may be got back."

The soldier's wife, having climbed down from the oven, continued to implore me to take steps to get her husband back. I told her it was impossible, and asked what property her husband had left behind with his brother, to keep her and the children. There was none. He had handed over his land to his brother, that he might feed her and the children. They had had three sheep; but two had been sold to pay the expenses of getting her husband off, and there was only some old rubbish left, she said, besides a sheep and two fowls. That was all she had. Her mother-in-law confirmed her words.

I asked the soldier's wife where she had come from. She came from Sergíevskoe. Sergíevskoe is a large, well-to-do village some thirty miles off. I asked if her parents were alive. She said they were alive, and living comfortably.

"Why should you not go to them?" I asked.

"I thought of that myself, but am afraid they won't have the four of us."

"Perhaps they will. Why not write to them? Shall I write for you?"

The woman agreed, and I noted down her parents' address.

While I was talking to the woman, the eldest child—a fat-bellied girl—

came up to her mother, and, pulling at her sleeve, began asking for something, probably food. The woman went on talking to me, and paid no attention to the girl, who again pulled and muttered something.

"There's no getting rid of you!" exclaimed the woman, and with a swing of her arm struck her on the head. The girl burst into a howl.

Having finished my business there, I left the hut and went back to the widow.

She was outside her house, waiting for me, and again asked me to come and look at her calf. I went in, and in the passage there really was a calf. The widow asked me to look at it. I did so, feeling that she was so engrossed in her calf that she could not imagine that anyone could help being interested in seeing it.

Having looked at the calf, I stepped inside, and asked:

"Where is the old woman?"

"The old woman?" the widow repeated, evidently surprised that after having seen the calf, I could still be interested in the old woman. "Why, on the top of the oven! Where else should she be?"

I went up to the oven, and greeted the old woman.

"Oh! ... oh!" answered a hoarse, feeble voice. "Who is it?"

I told her, and asked how she was getting on.

"What's my life worth?"

"Are you in pain?"

"Everything aches! Oh! ... oh!"

"The doctor is here with me; shall I call him in?"

"Doctor!... Oh! ... oh! What do I want with your doctor?... My doctor is up there.... Oh! ... oh!"

"She's old, you know," said the widow.

"Not older than I am," replied I.

"Not older? Much older! People say she is ninety," said the widow. "All her hair has come out. I cut it all off the other day."

"Why did you do that?"

"Why, it had nearly all come out, so I cut it off!"

"Oh! ... oh!" moaned the old woman; "oh! God has forgotten me! He does not take my soul. If the Lord won't take it, it can't go of itself! Oh! ... oh! It must be for my sins! ... I've nothing to moisten my throat.... If only I had a drop of tea to drink before I die.... Oh! ... oh!"

The doctor entered the hut, and I said goodbye and went out into the street.

We got into the sledge, and drove to a small neighbouring village to see the doctor's last patient, who had sent for him the day before. We went into the hut together.

The room was small, but clean; in the middle of it a cradle hung from the ceiling, and a woman stood rocking it energetically. At the table sat a girl of about eight, who gazed at us with surprised and frightened eyes.

"Where is he?" the doctor asked.

"On the oven," replied the woman, not ceasing to rock the cradle.

The doctor climbed up, and, leaning over the patient, did something to him.

I drew nearer, and asked about the sick man's condition.

The doctor gave me no answer. I climbed up, too, and gazing through the darkness gradually began to discern the hairy head of the man on the oven-top. Heavy, stifling air hung about the sick man, who lay on his back. The doctor was holding his left hand to feel the pulse.

"Is he very bad?" I asked.

Without answering me, the doctor turned to the woman.

"Light a lamp," he said.

She called the girl, told her to rock the cradle, and went and lit a lamp and handed it to the doctor. I got down, so as not to be in his way. He took the lamp, and continued to examine the patient.

The little girl, staring at us, did not rock the cradle strongly enough, and the baby began to cry piercingly and piteously. The mother, having handed the lamp to the doctor, pushed the girl angrily aside and again began to rock the cradle.

I returned to the doctor, and again asked how the patient was. The doctor, still occupied with the patient, softly whispered one word.

I did not hear, and asked again.

"The death-agony," he repeated, purposely using a non-Russian word, and got down and placed the lamp on the table.

The baby did not cease crying in a piteous and angry voice.

"What's that? Is he dead?" said the woman, as if she had understood the foreign word the doctor had used.

"Not yet, but there is no hope!" replied he.

"Then I must send for the priest," said the woman in a dissatisfied voice, rocking the screaming baby more and more violently.

"If only my husband was at home!... But now, who can I send? They've all gone to the forest for firewood."

"I can do nothing more here," said the doctor; and we went away.

I heard afterwards that the woman found someone to send for the priest, who had just time to administer the Sacrament to the dying man.

We drove home in silence, both, I think, experiencing the same feeling.

"What was the matter with him?" I asked at length.

"Inflammation of the lungs. I did not expect it to end so quickly. He had a very strong constitution, but the conditions were deadly. With 105 degrees of fever, he went and sat outside the hut, where there were only 20 degrees."

Again we drove on in silence for a long time.

"I noticed no bedding or pillow on the oven," said I.

"Nothing!" replied the doctor. And, evidently knowing what I was thinking about, he went on:

"Yesterday I was at Kroutoe to see a woman who has had a baby. To examine her properly, as was necessary, she should have been placed so that she could lie stretched out full length; but there was no place in the whole hut where that could be done."

Again we were silent, and again we probably both had the same thoughts. We reached home in silence. At the porch stood a fine pair of horses, harnessed tandem to a carpet-upholstered sledge. The handsome coachman was dressed in a sheepskin coat, and wore a thick fur cap. They belonged to my son, who had driven over from his estate.

And here we are sitting at the dinner-table, laid for ten persons. One of the places is empty. It is my little granddaughter's. She is not quite well to-day, and is having her dinner in her room with her nurse. A specially hygienic dinner has been prepared for her: beef-tea and sago.

At our big dinner of four courses, with two kinds of wine, served by two footmen, and eaten at a table decorated with flowers, this is the kind of talk that goes on:

"Where do these splendid roses come from?" asks my son.

My wife tells him that a lady, who will not divulge her name, sends them from Petersburg.

"Roses like these cost three shillings each," says my son, and goes on to relate how at some concert or play such roses were showered on a performer till they covered the stage. The conversation passes on to music, and then to a man who is a very good judge and patron of music.

"By the by, how is he?"

"Oh, he is always ailing. He is again going to Italy. He always spends the winter there, and his health improves wonderfully."

"But the journey is very trying and tedious."

"Oh no! Not if one takes the express—it is only thirty-nine hours."

"All the same, it is very dull."

"Wait a bit! We shall fly before long!"

THIRD DAY-TAXES

Besides my ordinary visitors and applicants, there are to-day some special ones. The first is a childless old peasant who is ending his life in great poverty. The second is a poor woman with a crowd of children. The third is, I believe, a well-to-do peasant.

All three have come from our village, and all have come about the same business. The taxes are being collected before the New Year, and the old man's samovár, the woman's only sheep, and one of the well-to-do peasant's cows, have been noted down for seizure in case of non-payment. They all ask me to defend them or assist them, or to do both.

The well-to-do peasant, a tall, handsome, elderly man, is the first to speak. He tells me that the Village Elder came, noted down the cow, and demands twenty-seven roubles. This levy is for the obligatory Grain Reserve Fund, and ought not, the peasant thinks, to be collected at this time of year. I know nothing about it, and tell him that I will inquire in the District Government Office, and will let him know whether the payment of the tax can be postponed or not.

The second to speak is the old man whose samovár has been noted. The small, thin, weakly, poorly clad man relates, with pathetic grief and bewilderment, how they came, took his samovár, and demanded three roubles and seventy copecks of him, which he has not got and can't get.

I ask him what the tax is for.

"Some kind of Government tax.... Who can tell what it is? Where am I and my old woman to get the money? As it is, we hardly manage to live!... What kind of laws are these? Have pity on our old age, and help us somehow!"

I promise to inquire, and to do what I can, and I turn to the woman. She is thin and worn-out. I know her, and know that her husband is a drunkard, and that she has five children.

"They have seized my sheep! They come and say: 'Pay the money!' 'My husband is away, working,' I say. 'Pay up!' say they. But where am I to find it? I only had one sheep, and they are taking it!" And she begins to cry.

I promise to find out, and to help her if I can. First, I go to the Village Elder, to find out what the taxes are, and why they are collecting them so rigorously.

In the village street, two other petitioners stop me. Their husbands are away at work. One asks me to buy some of her home-woven linen, and offers it for two roubles. "Because they have seized my hens! I had just reared them, and live by selling the eggs. Do buy it; it is good linen! I would not let it go for three roubles if I were not in great need!"

I send her away, promising to consider matters when I return—perhaps I may be able to arrange about the tax.

Before I reach the Elder's house, a woman comes to meet me: a quick-eyed, black-eyed ex-pupil of mine—Ólga, now already an old woman. She is in the same plight: they have seized her calf.

I come to the Elder. He is a strong, intelligent-looking peasant, with a grizzly beard. He comes out into the street to me. I ask him what taxes are being collected, and why so rigorously. He replies that he has had very strict orders to get in all arrears before the New Year.

"Have you had orders to confiscate samovárs and cattle?"

"Of course!" replies the Village Elder, shrugging his shoulders. "The taxes must be paid.... Take Abakoúmof now, for instance," said he, referring to the well-to-do peasant whose cow had been taken in payment of some Grain Reserve Fund. "His son is an isvóstchik: they have three horses. Why shouldn't he pay? He's always trying to get out of it."

"Well, suppose it so in his case," say I; "but how about those who are really poor?" And I name the old man whose samovár they are taking.

"Yes; they really are poor, and have nothing to pay with. But just as if such things get considered up there!"

I name the woman whose sheep was taken. The Elder is sorry for her too, but, as if excusing himself, explains that he must obey orders.

I inquire how long he has been an Elder, and what pay he gets.

"How much do I get?" he says, replying not to the question I ask, but to the question in my mind, which he guesses namely, why he takes part in such proceedings. "Well, I do want to resign! We get thirty roubles a month, but are obliged to do things that are wrong."

"Well, and will they really confiscate the samovárs and sheep and fowls?" I ask.

"Why, of course! We are bound to take them, and the District Government will arrange for their sale."

"And will the things be sold?"

"The folk will manage to pay up somehow."

I go to the woman who came to me about her sheep. Her hut is tiny, and in the passage outside is her only sheep, which is to go to support the Imperial Budget. Seeing me, she, a nervous woman worn out by want and overwork, begins to talk excitedly and rapidly, as peasant women do.

"See how I live! They're taking my last sheep, and I myself and these brats are barely alive!" She points up at the bunks and the oven-top, where her children are. "Come down!... Now then, don't be frightened!... There now, how's one to keep oneself and them naked brats?"

The brats, almost literally naked, with nothing on but tattered shirts—not even any trousers—climb down from the oven and surround their mother.

The same day I go to the District Office, to make inquiries about this way of exacting taxation, which is new to me.

The District Elder is not in. He will be back soon. In the Office several persons are standing behind the grating, also waiting to see him.

I ask them who they are, and what they have come about. Two of them have come to get passports, in order to be able to go out to work at a distance. They have brought money to pay for the passports. Another has come to get a copy of the District Court's decision rejecting his petition that the homestead—where he has lived and worked for twenty-three years, and which has belonged to his uncle, who adopted him,—now that his uncle and aunt are dead, should not be taken from him by his uncle's granddaughter. She, being the direct heiress, and taking advantage of the law of the 9th November, is selling the freehold of the land and homestead on which the petitioner lived. His petition has been rejected, but he cannot believe that this is the law, and wants to appeal to some higher Court—though he does not know what Court. I explain that there is such a law, and this provokes disapproval, amounting to perplexity and incredulity, among all those who are present.

Hardly have I finished talking with this man, when a tall peasant with a stern, severe face asks me for an explanation of his affairs. The business he has come about is this: he and his fellow villagers have, from time immemorial, been getting iron ore from their land; and now a decree has been published prohibiting this. "Not dig on one's own land? What laws are these? We only live by digging the iron! We have been trying for more than a month, and can't get anything settled. We don't know what to think of it; they'll ruin us completely, and that will be the end of the matter!"

I can say nothing comforting to this man, and turn to the Elder—who has just come back—to inquire about the vigorous measures which are being taken to exact payment of arrears of taxation in our village. I ask under what clauses of the Act the taxes are being levied. The Elder tells me that there are seven different kinds of rates and taxes, the arrears of all of which are now being collected from the peasants: (1) the Imperial Taxes, (2) the Local Government Taxes, (3) the Insurance Taxes, (4) the arrears of Former Grain Reserve Funds, (5) New Grain Reserve Funds in lieu of contributions in kind, (6) Communal and District Taxes, and (7) Village Taxes.

The District Elder tells me, as the Village Elder had done, that the taxes were being collected with special rigour by order of the higher authorities. He admits that it is no easy task to collect the taxes from the poor, but he shows less sympathy than the Village Elder did. He does not venture to censure the authorities; and, above all, he has hardly any doubt of the usefulness of his office, or of the rightness of taking part in such activity.

"One can't, after all, encourage...."

Soon after, I had occasion to talk about these things with a Zémsky Natchálnik.[3] He had very little compassion for the hard lot of the poverty-stricken folk whom he scarcely ever saw, and just as little doubt of the morality and lawfulness of his activity. In his conversation with me he admitted that, on the whole, it would be pleasanter not to serve at all; but he considered himself a useful functionary, because other men in his place would do even worse things. "And once one is living in the country, why not take the salary, small as it is, of a Zémsky Natchálnik?"

The views of a Governor on the collection of taxes necessary to meet the needs of those who are occupied in arranging for the nation's welfare, were entirely free from any considerations as to samovárs, sheep, homespun linen, or calves taken from the poorest inhabitants of the villages; and he had not the slightest doubt as to the usefulness of his activity.

And finally, the Ministers and those who are busy managing the liquor traffic, those who are occupied in teaching men to kill one another, and those who are engaged in condemning people to exile, to prison, to penal servitude, or to the gallows—all the Ministers and their assistants are quite convinced that samovárs and sheep and linen and calves taken from beggars, are put to their best use in producing vódka (which poisons the people), weapons for killing men, the erection of gaols and lock-ups, and, among other things, in paying to them and to their assistants the salaries they require to furnish drawing-rooms, to buy dresses for their wives, and for journeys and amusements which they undertake as relaxations after fulfilling their arduous labours for the welfare of the coarse and ungrateful masses.

CONCLUSION-A DREAM

A few nights ago I dreamt so significant a dream that several times during the following day I asked myself, "What has happened to-day that is so specially important?" And then I remembered that the specially important thing was what I had seen, or rather heard, in my dream.

It was a speech that struck me greatly, spoken by one who, as often happens in dreams, was a combination of two men: my old friend, now dead, Vladímir Orlóf, with grey curls on each side of his bald head, and Nicholas Andréyevitch, a copyist who lived with my brother.

The speech was evoked by the conversation of a rich lady, the hostess, with a landowner who was visiting her house. The lady had recounted how the peasants on a neighbouring estate had burnt the landlord's house and several sheds which sheltered century-old cherry trees and duchesse pears. Her visitor, the landowner, related how the peasants had cut down some oaks in his forest, and had even carted away a stack of hay.

"Neither arson nor robbery is considered a crime nowadays. The immorality of our people is terrible: they have all become thieves!" said someone.

And in answer to those words, that man, combined of two, spoke as follows:

"The peasants have stolen oaks and hay, and are thieves, and the most immoral class," he began, addressing no one in particular. "Now, in the Caucasus, a chieftain used to raid the Aouls and carry off all the horses of the inhabitants. But one of them found means to get back from the chieftain's herds at least one of the horses that had been stolen from him. Was that man a thief, because he got back one of the many horses stolen from him? And is it not the same with the trees, the grass, the hay, and all the rest of the things you say the peasants have stolen from you? The earth is the Lord's, and common to all; and if the peasants have taken what was grown on the common land of which they have been deprived, they have not stolen, but have only resumed possession of a small part of what has been stolen from them.

"I know you consider land to be the property of the landlord, and therefore call the restoration to themselves of its produce by the peasants—robbery; but, you know, that is not true! The land never was, and never can be, anyone's property. If a man has more of it than he requires, while others have none, then he who possesses the surplus land possesses not land but men; and men cannot be the property of other men.

"Because a dozen mischievous lads have burnt some cherry tree sheds, and have cut down some trees, you say the peasants are thieves, and the most immoral class!...

"How can your tongue frame such words! They have stolen ten oaks from you. Stolen! 'To prison with them!'

"Why, if they had taken not your oaks alone but everything that is in this house, they would only have taken what is theirs: made by them and their brothers, but certainly not by you! 'Stolen oaks!' But for ages you have been stealing from them, not oaks but their lives, and the lives of their children, their womenfolk and their old men—who withered away before their time—only because they were deprived of the land God gave to them in common with all men, and they were obliged to work for you.

"Only think of the life those millions of men have lived and are living, and of how you live! Only consider what they do, supplying you with all the comforts of life, and of what you do for them, depriving them of everything—even of the possibility of supporting themselves and their families! All you live on—everything in this room, everything in this house, and in all your splendid cities, all your palaces, all your mad, literally mad, luxuries—has been made, and is still continually being made, by them.

"And they know this. They know that these parks of yours, and your race-horses, motor cars, palaces, dainty dishes and finery, and all the nastiness and stupidity you call 'science' and 'art'—are purchased with the lives of their brothers and sisters. They know and cannot help knowing this. Then think what feelings these people would have towards you, if they were like you!

"One would suppose that, knowing all you inflict on them, they could not but hate you from the bottom of their souls, and could not help wishing to revenge themselves on you. And you know there are tens of millions of them, and only some thousands of you. But what do they do?... Why, instead of crushing you as useless and harmful reptiles, they continue to repay your evil with good, and live their laborious and reasonable, though hard life, patiently biding the day when you will become conscious of your sin and will amend your ways. But instead of that, what do you do? From the height of your refined, self-confident immorality, you deign to stoop to those 'depraved, coarse people.' You enlighten them, and play the benefactor to them; that is to say, with the means supplied to you by their labour, you inoculate them with your depravity, and blame, correct, and best of all 'punish' them, as unreasoning or vicious infants bite the breasts that feed them.

"Yes, look at yourselves, and consider what you are and what they are! Realise that they alone live, while you, with your Doúmas, Ministries, Synods, Academies, Universities, Conservatoires, Law Courts, armies, and all such stupidities and nastinesses, are but playing at life, and spoiling it for yourselves and others. They, the people, are alive. They are the tree, and you are harmful growths—fungi on the plant. Realise, then, all your insignificance and their grandeur! Understand your sin, and try to repent, and at all costs set the people free...."

"How well he speaks!" thought I. "Can it be a dream?"

And as I thought that, I awoke.

This dream set me again thinking about the land question: a question of which those who live constantly in the country, among a poverty-stricken agricultural peasant population, cannot help thinking. I know I have often written about it; but under the influence of that dream, even at the risk of repeating myself, I once more felt the need to express myself. Carthago delenda est. As long as people's attitude towards private property in land remains unchanged, the cruelty, madness and evil of this form of the enslavement of some men by others, cannot be pointed out too frequently.

People say that land is property, and they say this because the Government recognises private property in land. But fifty years ago the Government upheld private property in human beings; yet a time came when it was admitted that human beings cannot be private property, and the Government ceased to hold them to be property. So it will be with property in land. The Government now upholds that property, and protects it by its power; but a day will come when the Government will cease to acknowledge this kind of property, and will abolish it. The Government will have to abolish it, because private property in land is just such an injustice as property in men—serfdom—used to be. The difference lies only in the fact that serfdom was a direct, definite slavery, while land-slavery is indirect and indefinite. Then Peter was John's slave, whereas now Peter is the slave of some person unknown, but certainly of him who owns the land Peter requires in order to feed himself and his family. And not only is land-slavery as unjust and cruel a slavery as serfdom used to be, it is even harder on the slaves, and more criminal on the part of the slave-holders. For under serfdom—if not from sympathy, then at least from self-interest—the owner was obliged to see to it that his serf did not wither away and die of want, but to the best of his ability and understanding he looked after his slaves' morality. Now the landowner cares nothing if his landless slave withers away or becomes demoralised; for he knows that however many men die or become depraved at his work, he will always be able to find workmen.

The injustice and cruelty of the new, present-day slavery—land-slavery—is so evident, and the condition of the slaves is everywhere so hard, that one would have expected this new slavery to have been recognised by this time as out of date, just as serfdom was admittedly out of date half a century ago; and it should, one would have thought, have been abolished, as serfdom was abolished.

"But," it is said, "property in land cannot be abolished, for it would be impossible to divide equally among all the labourers and non-labourers the advantages given by land of different qualities."

But that is not true. To abolish property in land, no distribution of land is necessary.

Just as, when serfdom was abolished, no distribution of the people liberated was necessary, but all that was needed was the abolition of the law that upheld serfdom, so with the abolition of private property in land: no distribution of land is needed, but only the abolition of the law sanctioning private property in land. And as when serfdom was abolished, the serfs of their own accord settled down as best suited them, so when private property in land is abolished, people will find a way of sharing the land among themselves so that all may have equal advantage from it. How this will be arranged, whether by Henry George's Single-Tax system, or in some other way, we cannot foresee. But it is certain that the Government need only cease to uphold by force the obviously unjust and oppressive rights of property in land, and the people, released from those restrictions, will always find means of apportioning the land by common consent, in such a way that everyone will have an equal share of the benefits the use of the land confers.

It is only necessary for the majority of land-owners—that is, slave-owners—to understand (as they did in the matter of serfdom) that property in land is as hard on the present-day slaves, and as great an iniquity on the part of the slave-owners, as serfdom was; and, having understood that, it is only necessary for them to impress on the Government the necessity of repealing the laws sanctioning property in land—that is, land-slavery. One would have thought that, as in the 'fifties, the best members of society (chiefly the serf-owning nobles themselves), having understood the criminality of their position, explained to the Government the necessity for abolishing their evidently out-of-date and immoral rights, and serfdom was abolished, so it should be now with regard to private property in land, which is land-slavery.

But strange to say, the present slave-owners, the landed proprietors, not only fail to see the criminality of their position, and do not impress on the Government the necessity of abolishing land-slavery, but on the contrary they consciously and unconsciously, by all manner of means, blind themselves and their slaves to the criminality of their position.

The reasons of this are: first, that serfdom in the 'fifties, being the plain, downright enslavement of man by man, ran too clearly counter to religious and moral feeling; while land-slavery is not a direct, immediate slavery, but is a form of slavery more hidden from the slaves, and especially from the slave-owners, by complicated governmental, social and economic institutions. And the second reason is that, while in the days of serfdom only one class were slave-owners, all classes, except the most numerous one—consisting of peasants who have too little land: labourers and working men—are slave-owners now. Nowadays nobles, merchants, officials, manufacturers, professors, teachers, authors, musicians, painters, rich peasants, rich men's servants, well-paid artisans, electricians, mechanics, etc., are all slave-owners of the peasants who have insufficient land, and of the unskilled workmen who—apparently as a result of most varied causes, but in reality as a result of one cause alone (the appropriation of land by the landed proprietors)—are obliged to give their labour and even their lives to those who possess the advantages land affords. These two reasons—that the new slavery is less evident than the old, and that the new slave-owners are much more numerous than the old ones—account for the fact that the slave-owners of our day do not see, and do not admit, the cruelty and criminality of their position, and do not free themselves from it.

The slave-owners of our day not only do not admit that their position is criminal, and do not try to escape from it, but are quite sure that property in land is a necessary institution, essential to the social order, and that the wretched condition of the working classes—which they cannot help noticing—results from most varied causes, but certainly not from the recognition of some people's right to own land as private property.

This opinion of land-owning, and of the causes of the wretched condition of the labourers, is so well established in all the leading countries of the Christian world—France, England, Germany, America, etc.—that with very rare exceptions it never occurs to their public men to look in the right direction for the cause of the wretched condition of the workers.

That is so in Europe and America; but one would have expected that for us Russians, with our hundred million peasant population who deny the principle of private ownership in land, and with our enormous tracts of land, and with the almost religious desire of our people for agricultural life, an answer very different to the general European answer to questions as to the causes of the distress among the workers, and as to the means of bettering their position, would naturally present itself.

One would think that we Russians might understand that if we really are concerned about, and desire to improve, the position of the people and to free them from the aggravating and demoralising fetters with which they are bound, the means to do this are indicated both by common-sense and by the voice of the people, and are simply—the abolition of private property in land, that is to say, the abolition of land-slavery.

But, strange to relate, in Russian society, occupied with questions of the improvement of the condition or the working classes, there is no suggestion of this one, natural, simple and self-evident means of improving their condition. We Russians, though our peasants' outlook on the land question is probably centuries ahead of the rest of Europe, can devise nothing better for the improvement of our people's condition than to establish among ourselves, on the European model, Doúmas, Councils, Ministries, Courts, Zémstvos, Universities, Extension Lectures, Academies, elementary schools, fleets, submarines, air-ships, and many other of the queerest things quite foreign to and unnecessary for the people, and we do not do the one thing that is demanded by religion, morality, and common-sense, as well as by the whole of the peasantry.

Nor is this all. While arranging the fate of our people, who do not and never did acknowledge land-ownership, we, imitating Europe, try in all sorts of cunning ways, and by deception, bribery, and even force, to accustom them to the idea of property in land—that is to say, we try to deprave them and to destroy their consciousness of the truth they have held for ages, and which sooner or later will certainly be acknowledged by the whole human race: the truth that all who live on the earth cannot but have an equal right to its use.

These efforts to inoculate the people with the idea of landed property that is so foreign to them, are unceasingly made, with great perseverance and zeal by the Government, and consciously or for the most part unconsciously, from an instinct of self-preservation, by all the slave-holders of our time. And the slave-holders of our time are not the land-owners alone, but are all those who, as a result of the people being deprived of the land, enjoy power over them.

Most strenuous efforts are made to deprave the people; but, thank God! it may be safely said that till now all those efforts have only had an effect on the smallest and worst part of Russia's peasant population. The many-millioned majority of Russian workmen who hold but little land and live—not the depraved, parasitic life of the slave-owners, but their own reasonable, hard-working lives—do not yield to those efforts; because for them the solution of the land question is not one of personal advantage, as it is regarded by all the different slave-owners of to-day. For the enormous majority of peasants, the solution of that problem is not arrived at by mutually contradictory economic theories that spring up to-day and to-morrow are forgotten, but is found in the one truth, which is realised by them, and always has been and is realised by all reasonable men the world over,—the truth that all men are brothers and have therefore all an equal right to all the blessings of the world and, among the rest, to the most necessary of all rights—namely, the equal right of all to the use of the land.

Living in this truth, an enormous majority of the peasants attach no importance to all the wretched measures adopted by the Government about this or that alteration of the laws of land-ownership, for they know that there is only one solution to the land question—the total abolition of private property in land, and of land-slavery. And, knowing this, they quietly await their day, which sooner or later must come.

SINGING IN THE VILLAGE

Voices and an accordion sounded as if close by, though through the mist nobody could be seen. It was a work-day morning, and I was surprised to hear music.

"Oh, it's the recruits' leave-taking," thought I, remembering that I had heard something a few days before about five men being drawn from our village. Involuntarily attracted by the merry song, I went in the direction whence it proceeded.

As I approached the singers, the sound of song and accordion suddenly stopped. The singers, that is the lads who were leave-taking, entered the double-fronted brick cottage belonging to the father of one of them. Before the door stood a small group of women, girls, and children.

While I was finding out whose sons were going, and why they had entered that cottage, the lads themselves, accompanied by their mothers and sisters, came out at the door. There were five of them: four bachelors and one married man. Our village is near the town where nearly all these conscripts had worked. They were dressed town-fashion, evidently wearing their best clothes: peajackets, new caps, and high, showy boots. Conspicuous among them was a young fellow, well built though not tall, with a sweet, merry, expressive face, a small beard and moustache just beginning to sprout, and bright hazel eyes. As he came out, he at once took a big, expensive-looking accordion that was hanging over his shoulders and, having bowed to me, started playing the merry tune of "Bárynya," running his fingers nimbly over the keys and keeping exact time, as he moved with rhythmic step jauntily down the road.

Beside him walked a thick-set, fair-haired lad, also of medium height. He looked gaily from side to side, and sang second with spirit, in harmony with the first singer. He was the married one. These two walked ahead of the other three, who were also well dressed, and not remarkable in any way except that one of them was tall.

Together with the crowd I followed the lads. All their songs were merry, and no expression of grief was heard while the procession was going along; but as soon as we came to the next house at which the lads were to be treated, the lamentations of the women began. It was difficult to make out what they were saying; only a word here and there could be distinguished: "death ... father and mother ... native land ..."; and after every verse, the woman who led the chanting took a deep breath, and burst out into long-drawn moans, followed by hysterical laughter. The women were the mothers and sisters of the conscripts. Beside the lamentations of these relatives, one heard the admonitions of their friends.

"Now then, Matryóna, that's enough! You must be tired out," I heard one woman say, consoling another who was lamenting.

The lads entered the cottage. I remained outside, talking with a peasant acquaintance, Vasíly Oréhof, a former pupil of mine. His son, one of the five, was the married man who had been singing second as he went along.

"Well," I said, "it is a pity!"

"What's to be done? Pity or not, one has to serve."

And he told me of his domestic affairs. He had three sons: the eldest was living at home, the second was now being taken, and a third (who, like the second, had gone away to work) was contributing dutifully to the support of the home. The one who was leaving had evidently not sent home much.

"He has married a townswoman. His wife is not fit for our work. He is a lopped-off branch and thinks only of keeping himself. To be sure it's a pity, but it can't be helped!"

While we were talking, the lads came out into the street, and the lamentations, shrieks, laughter, and adjurations recommenced. After standing about for some five minutes, the procession moved on with songs and accordion accompaniment. One could not help marvelling at the energy and spirit of the player, as he beat time accurately, stamped his foot, stopped short, and then after a pause again took up the melody most merrily, exactly on the right beat, while he gazed around with his kind, hazel eyes. Evidently he had a real and great talent for music.

I looked at him, and (so at least it seemed to me) he felt abashed when he met my eyes, and with a twitch of his brows he turned away, and again burst out with even more spirit than before. When we reached the fifth and last of the cottages, the lads entered, and I followed them. All five of them were made to sit round a table covered with a cloth, on which were bread and vódka. The host, the man I had been talking to, who was now to take leave of his married son, poured out the vódka and handed it round. The lads hardly drank at all (at most a quarter of a glass) or even handed it back after just raising it to their lips. The hostess cut some bread, and served slices round to eat with the vódka.

While I was looking at the lads, a woman, dressed in clothes that seemed to me strange and incongruous, got down from the top of the oven, close to where I sat. She wore a light green dress (silk, I think) with fashionable trimmings, and high-heeled boots. Her fair hair was arranged in quite the modern style, like a large round cap, and she wore big, ring-shaped, gold earrings. Her face was neither sad nor cheerful, but looked as if she were offended.

After getting down, she went out into the passage, clattering with the heels of her new boots and paying no heed to the lads. All about this woman—her clothing, the offended expression of her face, and above all her earrings—was so foreign to the surroundings that I could not understand how she had come to be on the top of Vasíly Oréhof's oven. I asked a woman sitting near me who she was.

"Vasíly's daughter-in-law; she has been a housemaid," was the answer.

The host began offering vódka a third time, but the lads refused, rose, said grace, thanked the hosts, and went out.

In the street, the lamentations recommenced at once. The first to raise her voice was a very old woman with a bent back. She lamented in such a peculiarly piteous voice, and wailed so, that the women kept soothing the sobbing, staggering old creature, and supported her by her elbows.

"Who is she?" I inquired.

"Why, it's his granny; Vasíly's mother, that is."

The old woman burst into hysterical laughter and fell into the arms of the women who supported her, and just then the procession started again, and again the accordion and the merry voices struck up their tune. At the end of the village the procession was overtaken by the carts which were to carry the conscripts to the District Office. The weeping and wailing stopped. The accordion-player, getting more and more elated, bending his head to one side and resting on one foot, turned out the toes of the other and stamped with it, while his fingers produced brilliant fioritures, and exactly at the right instant the bold, high, merry tones of his song, and the second of Vasíly's son, again chimed in. Old and young, and especially the children who surrounded the crowd, and I with them, fixed their eyes admiringly on the singer.

"He is clever, the rascal!" said one of the peasants.

"'Sorrow weeps, and sorrow sings!'" replied another.

At that moment one of the young fellows whom we were seeing off—the tall one—came up with long, energetic strides, and stooped to speak to the one who played the accordion.

"What a fine fellow," I thought; "they will put him in the Guards." I did not know who he was or what house he belonged to.

"Whose son is that one? That gallant fellow?" I asked a little old man, pointing to the fine lad.

The old man raised his cap and bowed to me, but did not hear my question.

"What did you say?" asked he.

I had not recognised him, but as soon as he spoke I knew him at once. He is a hard-working, good peasant who, as often happens, seems specially marked out for misfortune: first, two horses were stolen from him, then his house burnt down, and then his wife died. I had not seen Prokófey for a long time, and remembered him as a bright red-haired man of medium height; whereas he was now not red, but quite grey-haired, and small.

"Ah, Prokófey, it's you!" I said. "I was asking whose son that fine fellow is—that one who has just spoken to Alexander?"

"That one?" Prokófey replied, pointing with a motion of his head to the tall lad. He shook his head and mumbled something I did not understand.

"I'm asking whose son the lad is?" I repeated, and turned to look at Prokófey.

His face was puckered, and his jaw trembled.

"He's mine!" he muttered, and, turning away and hiding his face in his hand, began to whimper like a child.

And only then, after the two words, "He's mine!" spoken by Prokófey, did I realise, not only in my mind but in my whole being, the horror of what was taking place before my eyes that memorable misty morning. All the disjointed, incomprehensible, strange things I had seen suddenly acquired a simple, clear, and terrible significance. I became painfully ashamed of having looked on as at an interesting spectacle. I stopped, conscious of having acted ill, and I turned to go home.

And to think that these things are at the present moment being done to tens of thousands of men all over Russia, and have been done, and will long continue to be done, to the meek, wise, and saintly Russian people, who are so cruelly and treacherously deceived!

TRAVELLER AND PEASANT

[The interior of a peasant hut. An old Traveller is sitting on a bench, reading a book. A Peasant, the master of the hut, just home from his work, sits down to supper and asks the Traveller to share it. The Traveller declines. The Peasant eats, and when he has finished, rises, says grace, and sits down beside the old man.]

PEASANT. What brings you?...

TRAVELLER [taking off his spectacles and putting down his book]. There is no train till to-morrow. The station is crowded, so I asked your missis to let me stay the night with you, and she allowed it.

PEASANT. That's all right, you can stay.

TRAVELLER. Thank you!... Well, and how are you living nowadays?

PEASANT. Living? What's our life like?... As bad as can be!

TRAVELLER. How's that?

PEASANT. Why, because we've nothing to live on! Our life is so hard that if we wanted a worse one, we couldn't get it.... You see, there are nine of us in family; all want to eat, and I have only got in four bushels of corn. Try and live on that! Whether one likes it or not, one has to go and work for wages ... and when you look for a job, wages are down!... The rich do what they like with us. The people increase, but the land doesn't, and taxes keep piling up! There's rent, and the district tax, and the land tax, and the tax for bridges, and insurance, and police, and for the corn store ... too many to count! And there are the priests and the landlords.... They all ride on our backs, except those who are too lazy!

TRAVELLER. I thought the peasants were doing well nowadays.

PEASANT. So well, that we go hungry for days at a time!

TRAVELLER. The reason I thought so, was that they have taken to squandering so much money.

PEASANT. Squandering what money? How strange you talk!... Here are people starving to death, and you talk of squandering money!

TRAVELLER. But how is it? The papers say that 700 million roubles (and a million is a thousand thousands)—700 million were spent by the peasants on vódka last year.

PEASANT. Are we the only ones that drink? Just look at the priests.... Don't they swill first-rate? And the gentlefolk aren't behind-hand!

TRAVELLER. Still, that's only a small part. The greater part stills falls to the peasants.

PEASANT. What of that? Are we not to drink at all?

TRAVELLER. No; what I mean is that if 700 millions were squandered on vódka in one year it shows that life can't be so very hard.... 700 millions! It's no joke ... one can hardly imagine it!

PEASANT. But how can one do without it? We didn't start the custom, and it's not for us to stop it.... There are the Church feasts, and weddings, and memorial feasts, and bargains to be wetted with a drink.... Whether one likes it or not, one can't get on without it. It's the custom!

TRAVELLER. But there are people who never drink, and yet they manage to live! After all, there's not much good in it.

PEASANT. No good at all! Only evil!

TRAVELLER. Then one ought not to drink.

PEASANT. Well, anyhow, drink or no drink, we've nothing to live on! We've not enough land. If we had land we could at least live ... but there's none to be had.

TRAVELLER. No land to be had? Why, isn't there plenty of land? Wherever one looks, one sees land!

PEASANT. There's land, right enough, but it's not ours. Your elbow's not far from your mouth, but just you try to bite it!

TRAVELLER. Not yours! Whose is it, then?

PEASANT. Whose?... Whose, indeed! There's that fat-bellied devil over there ... he's seized 5000 acres. He has no family, but he's never satisfied, while we've had to give up keeping fowls—there's nowhere for them to run about! It's nearly time for us to stop keeping cattle, too ... we've no fodder for them; and if a calf, or maybe a horse, happens to stray into his field, we have to pay fines and give him our last farthing.

TRAVELLER. What does he want all that land for?

PEASANT. What does he want the land for? Why, of course, he sows and reaps and sells, and puts the money in the bank.

TRAVELLER. How can he plough a stretch like that, and get his harvest in?

PEASANT. You talk as if you were a child!... What's he got money for, if not to hire labourers?... It's they that do the ploughing and reaping.

TRAVELLER. These labourers are some of you peasants, I expect?

PEASANT. Some are from these parts, and some from elsewhere.

TRAVELLER. Anyway, they are peasants?

PEASANT. Of course they are!... the same as ourselves. Who but a peasant ever works? Of course they are peasants.

TRAVELLER. And if the peasants did not go and work for him...?

PEASANT. Go or stay, he wouldn't let us have it. If the land were to lie idle, he'd not part with it! Like the dog in the manger, that doesn't eat the hay himself and won't let others eat it!

TRAVELLER. But how can he keep his land? I suppose it stretches over some three or four miles? How can he watch it all?

PEASANT. How queer you talk! He himself lies on his back, and fattens his paunch; but he keeps watchmen!

TRAVELLER. And those watchmen, I dare say, are also peasants?

PEASANT. What else could they be? Of course they are!

TRAVELLER. So that the peasants work the rich man's land for him, and guard it for him from themselves?

PEASANT. But how can one help it?

TRAVELLER. Simply by not going to work for him, and not being his watchmen! Then the land would be free. The land is God's, and the people are God's; let him who needs it, plough and sow and gather in the harvest!

PEASANT. That is to say, you think we ought to strike? To meet that, my friend, they have the soldiers. They'd send their soldiers ... one, two, fire!... some would get shot, and others taken up. Soldiers give short shrift!

TRAVELLER. But is it not also the likes of you that are soldiers? Why should they shoot at their own fellows?

PEASANT. How can they help it? That's what the oath is for.

TRAVELLER. The oath? What oath?

PEASANT. Don't you understand? Aren't you a Russian?... The oath is—well, it's the oath!

TRAVELLER. It means swearing, doesn't it?

PEASANT. Well, of course! They swear by the Cross and by the Gospels, to lay down their life for their country.

TRAVELLER. Well, I think that should not be done.

PEASANT. What should not be done?

TRAVELLER. Taking the oath.

PEASANT. Not done? Why, the law demands it!

TRAVELLER. No, it is not in the Law. In the Law of Christ, it is plainly forbidden. He said: "Swear not at all."

PEASANT. Come now! What about the priests?

TRAVELLER [takes a book, looks for the place, and reads]: "It was said by them of old time, Thou shalt not forswear thyself, but I say unto you, Swear not at all.... But let your speech be, Yea, yea; nay, nay: and whatsoever is more than these is of the evil one" (Matthew v. 33). So, according to Christ's Law, you must not swear.

PEASANT. If there were no oath, there would be no soldiers.

TRAVELLER. Well, and what good are the soldiers?

PEASANT. What good?... But supposing other Tsars were to come and attack our Tsar ... what then?

TRAVELLER. If the Tsars quarrel, let them fight it out themselves.

PEASANT. Come! How could that be possible?

TRAVELLER. It's very simple. He that believes in God, no matter what you may tell him, will never kill a man.

PEASANT. Then why did the priest read out in church that war was declared, and the Reserves were to be ready?

TRAVELLER. I know nothing about that; but I know that in the Commandments, in the Sixth, it says quite plainly: "Thou shalt do no murder." You see, it is forbidden for a man to kill a man.

PEASANT. That means, at home! At the wars, how could you help it? They're enemies!

TRAVELLER. According to Christ's Gospel, there is no such thing as an enemy. You are told to love everybody.

[Opens the Bible and looks for place.

PEASANT. Well, read it!

TRAVELLER. "Ye have heard that it was said by them of old time, Thou shalt not kill; and whosoever shall kill shall be in danger of the judgment.... Ye have heard that it was said, Thou shalt love thy neighbour, and hate thine enemy: but I say unto you, Love your enemies, and pray for them that persecute you" (Matthew v. 21, 43-44).

[A long pause.

PEASANT. Well, but what about taxes? Ought we to refuse to pay them too?

TRAVELLER. That's as you think best. If your own children are hungry, naturally you should first feed them.

PEASANT. So you think soldiers are not wanted at all?

TRAVELLER. What good do they do? Millions and millions are collected from you and your folk for them—it's no joke to clothe and feed such a host! There are nearly a million of those idlers, and they're only useful to keep the land from you; and it is on you they will fire.

[The PEASANT sighs, and shakes his head.

PEASANT. That's true enough! If everybody were to do it at once ... but if one or two make a stand, they'll be shot or sent to Siberia, and that will be the end of the matter.

TRAVELLER. And yet there are men, even now—young men—who by themselves stand up for the Law of God, and refuse to serve. They say: "According to Christ's Law, I dare not be a murderer! Do as you please, but I won't take a rifle in my hands!"

PEASANT. Well, and what happens?

TRAVELLER. They are put in prison; they remain there, poor fellows, three years, or four.... But I've heard that it's not so bad for them, for the authorities themselves respect them. And some are even let out as unfit for service—bad health! Though he is sometimes a strapping, broad-shouldered fellow, he's "not fit," because they're afraid of taking a man of that kind, for fear he should tell others that soldiering is against God's Law. So they let him go.

PEASANT. Really?

TRAVELLER. Yes, sometimes it happens that they are let off; but it also happens that they die there. Still, soldiers die too, and even get maimed in service—lose a leg, or an arm....

PEASANT. Oh, you're a clever fellow! It would be a good thing, only it won't work out like that.

TRAVELLER. Why not?

PEASANT. That's why.

TRAVELLER. What's that?

PEASANT. That the authorities have power given them.

TRAVELLER. They only have power, because you obey them. Do not obey the authorities, and they won't have any power!

PEASANT. [shakes his head]. You do talk queer! How can one do without the authorities? It is quite impossible to do without some authority.

TRAVELLER. Of course it is! Only whom will you take for authority—the policeman, or God? Whom will you obey—the policeman, or God?

PEASANT. That goes without saying! No one is greater than God. To live for God is the chief thing.

TRAVELLER. Well, if you mean to live for God, you must obey God and not man. And if you live according to God, you will not drive people off the land: you will not be a policeman, a village elder, a tax-collector, a watchman, or above all, a soldier.... You will not promise to kill men.

PEASANT. And how about those long-maned fellows—the priests? They must see that things are being done not according to God's Law. Then why don't they teach how it ought to be?

TRAVELLER. I don't know anything about that. Let them go their way, and you go yours.

PEASANT. They are long-maned devils!

TRAVELLER. It's not right to judge others like that! We must each remember our own faults.

PEASANT. Yes, that's right enough. [Long pause. The PEASANT shakes his head, and smiles.] What it comes to is this: that if we all were to tackle it at once, the land would be ours at one go, and there would be no more taxes.

TRAVELLER. No, friend, that's not what I mean. I don't mean that if we live according to God's will, the land will be ours, and there will be no more taxes. I mean that our life is evil, only because we ourselves do evil. If one lived according to God's will, life would not be evil. What our life would be like if we lived according to God's will, God alone knows; but certainly life would not be evil. We drink, scold, fight, go to law, envy, and hate men; we do not accept God's Law; we judge others; call one fat-paunched and another long-maned; but if any one offers us money, we are ready to do anything for it: go as watchmen, policemen, or soldiers, to help ruin others, and to kill our own brothers. We ourselves live like devils, and yet we complain of others!

PEASANT. That's so! But it is hard, oh, how hard! Sometimes it's more than one can bear.

TRAVELLER. But, for our souls' sakes, we must bear it.

PEASANT. That's quite right.... We live badly, because we forget God.

TRAVELLER. Yes, that's it! That's why life is evil. Take the Revolutionaries; they say: "Let's kill this or that squire, or these fat-paunched rich folk (it's all because of them); and then our life will be happy." So they kill, and go on killing, and it profits them nothing. It's the same with the authorities: "Give us time!" they say, "and we'll hang, and do to death in the prisons, a thousand or a couple of thousand people, and then life will become good...." But it only gets worse and worse!

PEASANT. Yes, that's just it! How can judging and punishing do any good? It must be done according to God's Law.

TRAVELLER. Yes, that is just it. You must serve either God or the devil. If it's to be the devil, go and drink, scold, fight, hate, covet, don't obey God's Law, but man's laws, and life will be evil. If it is God, obey Him alone. Don't rob or kill, and don't even condemn, and do not hate any one. Do not plunge into evil actions, and then there will be no evil life.

PEASANT [sighs]. You speak well, daddy, very well—only we are taught so little! Oh, if we were taught more like that, things would be quite different! But people come from the town, and chatter about their way of bettering things: they chatter fine, but there's nothing in it.... Thank you, daddy, your words are good!... Well, where will you sleep? On the oven, yes?... The missis will make up a bed for you.

A TALK WITH A WAYFARER

I have come out early. My soul feels light and joyful. It is a wonderful morning. The sun is only just appearing from behind the trees. The dew glitters on them and on the grass. Everything is lovely; everyone is lovable. It is so beautiful that, as the saying has it, "One does not want to die." And, really, I do not want to die. I would willingly live a little longer in this world with such beauty around me and such joy in my heart. That, however, is not my affair, but the Master's....

I approach the village. Before the first house I see a man standing, motionless, sideways to me. He is evidently waiting for somebody or something, and waiting as only working people know how to wait, without impatience or vexation. I draw nearer: he is a bearded, strong, healthy peasant, with shaggy, slightly grey hair, and a simple, worker's face. He is smoking not a "cigar" twisted out of paper, but a short pipe. We greet one another.

"Where does old Alexéy live?" I ask.

"I don't know, friend; we are strangers here."

Not "I am a stranger," but "we are strangers." A Russian is hardly ever alone. If he is doing something wrong, he may perhaps say "I"; otherwise it is always "we" the family, "we" the artél, "we" the Commune.

"Strangers? Where do you come from?"

"We are from Kaloúga."

I point to his pipe. "And how much do you spend a year on smoking? Three or more roubles, I daresay!"

"Three? That would hardly be enough."

"Why not give it up?"

"How can one give it up when one's accustomed to it?"

"I also used to smoke, but have given it up ... and I feel so well—so free!"

"Well of course ... but it's dull without it."

"Give it up, and the dulness will go! Smoking is no good, you know!"

"No good at all."

"If it's no good, you should not do it. Seeing you smoke, others will do the same ... especially the young folk. They'll say, 'If the old folk smoke, God himself bids us do it!'"

"That's true enough."

"And your son, seeing you smoke, will do it too."

"Of course, my son too...."

"Well then, give it up!"

"I would, only it's so dull without it.... It's chiefly from dulness. When one feels dull, one has a smoke. That's where the mischief lies.... It's dull! At times it's so dull ... so dull ... so dull!" drawled he.

"The best remedy for that is to think of one's soul."

He threw a glance at me, and at once the expression of his face quite changed: instead of his former kindly, humorous, lively and talkative expression, he became attentive and serious.

"'Think of the soul ... of the soul,' you say?" he asked, gazing questioningly into my eyes.

"Yes! When you think of the soul, you give up all foolish things."

His face lit up affectionately.

"You are right, daddy! You say truly. To think of the soul is the great thing. The soul's the chief thing...." He paused. "Thank you, daddy, it is quite true"; and he pointed to his pipe. "What is it?... Good-for-nothing rubbish! The soul's the chief thing!" repeated he. "What you say is true," and his face grew still kindlier and more serious.

I wished to continue the conversation, but a lump rose in my throat (I have grown very weak in the matter of tears), and I could not speak. With a joyful, tender feeling I took leave of him, swallowing my tears, and I went away.

Yes, how can one help being joyful, living amid such people? How can one help expecting from such people all that is most excellent?

FROM THE DIARY

I am again staying with my friend, Tchertkóff, in the Moscow Government, and am visiting him now for the same reason that once caused us to meet on the border of the Orlóf Government, and that brought me to the Moscow Government a year ago. The reason is that Tchertkóff is allowed to live anywhere in the whole world, except in Toúla Government. So I travel to different ends of it to see him.

Before eight o'clock I go out for my usual walk. It is a hot day. At first I go along the hard clay road, past the acacia bushes already preparing to crack their pods and shed their seeds; then past the yellowing rye-field, with its still fresh and lovely cornflowers, and come out into a black fallow field, now almost all ploughed up. To the right an old man, in rough peasant-boots, ploughs with a sohá[4] and a poor, skinny horse; and I hear an angry old voice shout: "Gee-up!" and, from time to time, "Now, you devil!" and again, "Gee-up, devil!" I want to speak with him; but when I pass his furrow, he is at the other end of the field. I go on. There is another ploughman further on. This one I shall probably meet when he reaches the road. If so, I'll speak to him, if there is a chance. And we do meet just as he reaches the road.

He ploughs with a proper plough, harnessed to a big roan horse, and is a well-built young lad, well clad, and wearing good boots; and he answers my greeting of "God aid you!" pleasantly.

The plough does not cut into the hard, beaten track that crosses the field, and he lifts it over and halts.

"You find the plough better than a sohá?"

"Why, certainly ... much easier!"

"Have you had it long?"

"Not long—and it nearly got stolen...."

"But you got it back?"

"Yes! One of our own villagers had it."

"Well, and did you have the law of him?"

"Why, naturally!"

"But why prosecute, if you got the plough back?"

"Why, you see, he's a thief!"

"What then? The man will go to prison, and learn to steal worse!"

He looks at me seriously and attentively, evidently neither agreeing nor contradicting this, to him, new idea.

He has a fresh, healthy, intelligent face, with hair just appearing on his chin and upper lip, and with intelligent grey eyes.

He leaves the plough, evidently wishing to have a rest, and inclined for a talk. I take the plough-handles, and touch the perspiring, well-fed, full-grown mare. She presses her weight into her collar, and I take a few steps. But I do not manage the plough, the share jumps out of the furrow, and I stop the horse.

"No, you can't do it."

"I have only spoilt your furrow."

"That doesn't matter—I'll put it right!"

He backs his horse, to plough the part I have missed, but does not go on ploughing.

"It is hot in the sun.... Let's go and sit under the bushes," says he, pointing to a little wood just across the field.

We go into the shade of the young birches. He sits down on the ground, and I stop in front of him.

"What village are you from?"

"From Botvínino."

"Is that far?"

"There it is, shimmering on the hill," says he, pointing.

"Why are you ploughing so far from home?"

"This is not my land: it belongs to a peasant here. I have hired myself out to him."

"Hired yourself out for the whole summer?"

"No—to plough this ground twice, and sow it, all properly."

"Has he much land, then?"

"Yes, he sows about fifteen bushels of seed."

"Does he! And is that horse your own? It's a good horse."

"Yes, it's not a bad mare," he answers, with quiet pride.

The mare really is, in build, size, and condition, such as a peasant rarely possesses.

"I expect you are in service somewhere, and do carting?"

"No, I live at home. I'm my own master!"

"What, so young?"

"Yes! I was left fatherless at seven. My brother works at a Moscow factory. At first my sister helped; she also worked at a factory. But since I was fourteen I've had no help in all my affairs, and have worked and earned," says he, with calm consciousness of his dignity.

"Are you married?"

"No."

"Then, who does your housework?"

"Why, mother!"

"And you have a cow?"

"Two cows."

"Have you, really?... And how old are you?" I ask.

"Eighteen," he replies, with a slight smile, understanding that it interests me to see that so young a fellow has been able to manage so well. This, evidently, pleases him.

"How young you still are!" I say. "And will you have to go as a soldier?"

"Of course ... be conscripted!" says he, with the calm expression with which people speak of old age, death, and in general of things it is useless to argue about, because they are unavoidable.

As always happens now when one speaks to peasants, our talk touches on the land, and, describing his life, he says he has not enough land, and that if he did not do wage-labour, sometimes with and sometimes without his horse, he would not have anything to live on. But he says this with merry, pleased and proud self-satisfaction; and again remarks that he was left alone, master of the house, when he was fourteen, and has earned everything himself.

"And do you drink vódka?"

He evidently does not like to say that he does, and still does not wish to tell a lie.

"I do," he says, softly, shrugging his shoulders.

"And can you read and write?"

"Very well."

"And haven't you read books about strong drink?"

"No, I haven't."

"Well, but wouldn't it be better not to drink at all?"

"Of course. Little good comes of it."

"Then why not give it up?"

He is silent, evidently understanding, and thinking it over.

"It can be done, you know," say I, "and what a good thing it would be!... The day before yesterday I went to Ívino. When I reached one of the houses, the master came out to greet me, calling me by name. It turned out that we had met twelve years before.... It was Koúzin—do you know him?"

"Of course I do! Sergéy Timoféevitch, you mean?"

I tell him how we started a Temperance Society twelve years ago with Koúzin, who, though he used to drink, has quite given it up, and now tells me he is very glad to be rid of so nasty a habit; and, one sees, is living well, with his house and everything well managed, and who, had he not given up drinking, would have had none of these things.

"Yes, that is so!"

"Well then, you know, you should do the same. You are such a nice, good lad.... What do you need vódka for, when you say yourself there is no good in it?... You, too, should give it up!... It would be such a good thing!"

He remains silent, and looks at me intently. I prepare to go, and hold out my hand to him.

"Truly, give it up from now! It would be such a good thing!"

With his strong hand he firmly presses mine, evidently regarding my gesture as challenging him to promise.

"Very well then ... it can be done!" says he, quite unexpectedly, and in a joyous and resolute tone.

"Do you really promise?" say I, surprised.

"Well, of course! I promise," he says, nodding his head and smiling slightly.

The quiet tone of his voice, and his serious, attentive face, show that he is not joking, but that he is really making a promise he means to keep.

Old age or illness, or both together, has made me very ready to cry when I am touched with joy. The simple words of that kindly, firm, strong man, so evidently ready for all that is good, and standing so alone, touch me so that sobs rise to my throat, and I step aside, unable to utter a word.

After going a few steps, I regain control of myself, and turn to him and say (I have already asked his name):

"Mind, Alexander! ... the proverb says, 'Be slow to promise, but having promised, keep it!'"

"Yes, that's so. It will be safe."

I have seldom experienced a more joyful feeling than I had when I left him.

I have omitted to say that during our talk I had offered to give him some leaflets on drink and some booklets. [A man in a neighbouring village posted up one of those same leaflets on the wall outside his house lately, but it was pulled down and destroyed by the policeman.] He thanked me, and said he would come and fetch them in the dinner-hour.

He did not come in the dinner-hour, and I, sinner that I am, suspected that our whole conversation was not so important to him as it seemed to me, and that he did not want the books, and that, in general, I had attributed to him what was not in him. But he came in the evening, all perspiring from his work and from the walk. After finishing his work, he had ridden home, put up the plough, attended to his horse, and had now come a quarter of a mile to fetch the books.

I was sitting, with some visitors, on a splendid veranda, looking out on to flower-beds with ornamental vases on flower-set mounds—in short, in luxurious surroundings such as one is always ashamed of when one enters into human relations with working people.

I went out to him, and at once asked, "Have you not changed your mind? Will you really keep your promise?"

And again, with the same kindly smile, he replied, "Of course!... I have already told mother. She's glad, and thanks you."

I saw a bit of paper behind his ear.

"You smoke?"

"I do," he said, evidently expecting that I should begin persuading him to leave that off too. But I did not try to.

He remained silent; and then, by some strange connection of thoughts (I think he saw the interest I felt in his life, and wished to tell me of the important event awaiting him in the autumn) he said:

"But I did not tell you.... I am already betrothed...."

And he smiled, looking questioningly into my eyes. "It's to be in the autumn!"

"Really! That's a good thing! Where is she from?"

He told me.

"Has she a dowry?"

"No; what dowry should she have? But she's a good girl."

The idea came to me to put to him the question which always interests me when I come in contact with good young people of our day.

"Tell me," said I, "and forgive my asking—but please tell the truth: either do not answer at all, or tell the whole truth...."

He looked at me quietly and attentively.

"Why should I not tell you?"

"Have you ever sinned with a woman?"

Without a moment's hesitation, he replied simply:

"God preserve me! There's been nothing of the sort!"

"That's good, very good!" said I. "I am glad for you."

There was nothing more to say just then.

"Well then, I will fetch you the books, and God's help be with you!"

And we took leave of one another.

Yes, what a splendid, fertile soil on which to sow, and what a dreadful sin it is to cast upon it the seeds of falsehood, violence, drunkenness and profligacy!

FOOTNOTES:

[1] Not in the English sense, for there is no Poor-Law system entitling the destitute to demand maintenance.

[2] One of the most depressing features of L. N. Tolstoy's environment is the large number of unemployed and beggars from the adjacent highway. They wait outside the house for hours every day for the coming of Leo Nikolayevich. The consciousness of his inability to render them substantial aid weighs heavily upon him, as does also the fact that, owing to insurmountable obstacles, he cannot even feed them, and allow them to sleep in the house in which he himself lives. These unfortunates surround Leo Nikolayevich at the steps, and besiege him with their importunate requests, just at the time when he seeks the fresh air and is most in need of mental rest and solitude after long-continued and strenuous mental labour. In view of this fact, the idea has occurred to some of Leo Nikolayevich's friends, of establishing in the village of Yásnaya Polyána a lodging- and eating-house for tramps, the use of which by the latter would save L. N. unnecessary trouble. The establishment of such premises—L. N. has viewed the idea very favourably—would at least afford some temporary relief to the wandering poor who are in dire need. At the same time the peasantry of Yásnaya Polyána would be relieved of the too heavy burden of supporting the passing unemployed described by Tolstoy in his article. Lastly, it would afford Tolstoy, in his declining years, considerable mental relief, which it would seem that he has more than deserved by his incessant labours on behalf of distressed mankind. Perhaps among those who read the present sketches some will be found who, prompted by the impulses animating the author, may desire to render some material help towards the practical realisation of the projected undertaking.

Contributions may be sent to the following address: V. Tchertkoff, Editor of the Free Age Press, Christchurch, Hants, Eng.

[3] A Zémsky Natchálnik is a salaried official placed in authority in a district. He is often selected from among the local gentry, and wields very considerable authority.

[4] A primitive plough used by the peasants.

About Author

In the 1870s Tolstoy experienced a profound moral crisis, followed by what he regarded as an equally profound spiritual awakening, as outlined in his non-fiction work A Confession (1882). His literal interpretation of the ethical teachings of Jesus, centering on the Sermon on the Mount, caused him to become a fervent Christian anarchist and pacifist. Tolstoy's ideas on nonviolent resistance, expressed in such works as The Kingdom of God Is Within You (1894), were to have a profound impact on such pivotal 20th-century figures as Mahatma Gandhi and Martin Luther King Jr. Tolstoy also became a dedicated advocate of Georgism, the economic philosophy of Henry George, which he incorporated into his writing, particularly Resurrection (1899).

Origins

The Tolstoys were a well-known family of old Russian nobility who traced their ancestry to a mythical nobleman named Indris described by Pyotr Tolstoy as arriving "from Nemec, from the lands of Caesar" to Chernigov in 1353 along with his two sons Litvinos (or Litvonis) and Zimonten (or Zigmont) and a druzhina of 3000 people. While the word "Nemec" has been long used to describe Germans only, at that time it was applied to any foreigner who didn't speak Russian (from the word nemoy meaning mute). Indris was then converted to Eastern Orthodoxy under the name of Leonty and his sons – as Konstantin and Feodor, respectively. Konstantin's grandson Andrei Kharitonovich was nicknamed Tolstiy (translated as fat) by Vasily II of Moscow after he moved from Chernigov to Moscow.

Because of the pagan names and the fact that Chernigov at the time was ruled by Demetrius I Starshy some researches concluded that they were Lithuanians who arrived from the Grand Duchy of Lithuania, then part of the State of the Teutonic Order. At the same time, no mention of Indris was ever found in the 14th – 16th-century documents, while the Chernigov Chronicles used by Pyotr Tolstoy as a reference were lost. The first documented members of the Tolstoy family also lived during the 17th century, thus Pyotr

Tolstoy himself is generally considered the founder of the noble house, being granted the title of count by Peter the Great.

Life and career

Tolstoy was born at Yasnaya Polyana, a family estate 12 kilometres (7.5 mi) southwest of Tula, Russia, and 200 kilometers (120 mi) south of Moscow. He was the fourth of five children of Count Nikolai Ilyich Tolstoy (1794–1837), a veteran of the Patriotic War of 1812, and Countess Mariya Tolstaya (née Volkonskaya; 1790–1830). After his mother died when he was two and his father when he was nine, Tolstoy and his siblings were brought up by relatives. In 1844, he began studying law and oriental languages at Kazan University, where teachers described him as "both unable and unwilling to learn." Tolstoy left the university in the middle of his studies, returned to Yasnaya Polyana and then spent much of his time in Moscow, Tula and Saint Petersburg, leading a lax and leisurely lifestyle. He began writing during this period, including his first novel Childhood, a fictitious account of his own youth, which was published in 1852. In 1851, after running up heavy gambling debts, he went with his older brother to the Caucasus and joined the army. Tolstoy served as a young artillery officer during the Crimean War and was in Sevastopol during the 11-month-long siege of Sevastopol in 1854–55, including the Battle of the Chernaya. During the war he was recognised for his bravery and courage and promoted to lieutenant. He was appalled by the number of deaths involved in warfare, and left the army after the end of the Crimean War.

His conversion from a dissolute and privileged society author to the non-violent and spiritual anarchist of his latter days was brought about by his experience in the army as well as two trips around Europe in 1857 and 1860–61. Others who followed the same path were Alexander Herzen, Mikhail Bakunin and Peter Kropotkin. During his 1857 visit, Tolstoy witnessed a public execution in Paris, a traumatic experience that would mark the rest of his life. Writing in a letter to his friend Vasily Botkin: "The truth is that the State is a conspiracy designed not only to exploit, but above all to corrupt its citizens ... Henceforth, I shall never serve any government anywhere." Tolstoy's concept of non-violence or Ahimsa was bolstered when he read a

German version of the Tirukkural. He later instilled the concept in Mahatma Gandhi through his A Letter to a Hindu when young Gandhi corresponded with him seeking his advice.

His European trip in 1860–61 shaped both his political and literary development when he met Victor Hugo, whose literary talents Tolstoy praised after reading Hugo's newly finished Les Misérables. The similar evocation of battle scenes in Hugo's novel and Tolstoy's War and Peace indicates this influence. Tolstoy's political philosophy was also influenced by a March 1861 visit to French anarchist Pierre-Joseph Proudhon, then living in exile under an assumed name in Brussels. Apart from reviewing Proudhon's forthcoming publication, La Guerre et la Paix (War and Peace in French), whose title Tolstoy would borrow for his masterpiece, the two men discussed education, as Tolstoy wrote in his educational notebooks: "If I recount this conversation with Proudhon, it is to show that, in my personal experience, he was the only man who understood the significance of education and of the printing press in our time."

Fired by enthusiasm, Tolstoy returned to Yasnaya Polyana and founded 13 schools for the children of Russia's peasants, who had just been emancipated from serfdom in 1861. Tolstoy described the school's principles in his 1862 essay "The School at Yasnaya Polyana". Tolstoy's educational experiments were short-lived, partly due to harassment by the Tsarist secret police. However, as a direct forerunner to A.S. Neill's Summerhill School, the school at Yasnaya Polyana can justifiably be claimed the first example of a coherent theory of democratic education.

Towards the end of his career, Tolstoy was selected to receive the first Nobel Prize in Literature in 1901, but turned down the honor in October of the same year, worrying that the prize money would bring unwanted complications to his life.

Personal life

The death of his brother Nikolay in 1860 had an impact on Tolstoy, and led him to a desire to marry. On 23 September 1862, Tolstoy married Sophia Andreevna Behrs, who was 16 years his junior and the daughter of a court physician. She was called Sonya, the Russian diminutive of Sofia, by her family and friends. They had 13 children, eight of whom survived childhood:

Count Sergei Lvovich Tolstoy (1863–1947), composer and ethnomusicologist

Countess Tatyana Lvovna Tolstaya (1864–1950), wife of Mikhail Sergeevich Sukhotin

Count Ilya Lvovich Tolstoy (1866–1933), writer

Count Lev Lvovich Tolstoy (1869–1945), writer and sculptor

Countess Maria Lvovna Tolstaya (1871–1906), wife of Nikolai Leonidovich Obolensky

Count Peter Lvovich Tolstoy (1872–1873), died in infancy

Count Nikolai Lvovich Tolstoy (1874–1875), died in infancy

Countess Varvara Lvovna Tolstaya (1875–1875), died in infancy

Count Andrei Lvovich Tolstoy (1877–1916), served in the Russo-Japanese War

Count Michael Lvovich Tolstoy (1879–1944)

Count Alexei Lvovich Tolstoy (1881–1886)

Countess Alexandra Lvovna Tolstaya (1884–1979)

Count Ivan Lvovich Tolstoy (1888–1895)

The marriage was marked from the outset by sexual passion and emotional insensitivity when Tolstoy, on the eve of their marriage, gave her his diaries detailing his extensive sexual past and the fact that one of the serfs on his estate had borne him a son. Even so, their early married life was happy and allowed Tolstoy much freedom and the support system to compose War and Peace and Anna Karenina with Sonya acting as his secretary, editor, and financial manager. Sonya was copying and handwriting his epic works time after time. Tolstoy would continue editing War and Peace and had to have clean final drafts to be delivered to the publisher.

However, their later life together has been described by A.N. Wilson as one of the unhappiest in literary history. Tolstoy's relationship with his wife deteriorated as his beliefs became increasingly radical. This saw him seeking to reject his inherited and earned wealth, including the renunciation of the copyrights on his earlier works.

Some of the members of the Tolstoy family left Russia in the aftermath of the 1905 Russian Revolution and the subsequent establishment of the Soviet Union, and many of Leo Tolstoy's relatives and descendants today live in Sweden, Germany, the United Kingdom, France and the United States. Among them are Swedish jazz singer Viktoria Tolstoy and the Swedish landowner Christopher Paus, whose family owns the major estate Herresta outside Stockholm.

One of his great-great-grandsons, Vladimir Tolstoy (born 1962), is a director of the Yasnaya Polyana museum since 1994 and an adviser to the President of Russia on cultural affairs since 2012. Ilya Tolstoy's great-grandson, Pyotr Tolstoy, is a well-known Russian journalist and TV presenter as well as a State Duma deputy since 2016. His cousin Fyokla Tolstaya (born Anna Tolstaya in 1971), daughter of the acclaimed Soviet Slavist Nikita Tolstoy (ru) (1923–1996), is also a Russian journalist, TV and radio host.

Novels and fictional works

Tolstoy is considered one of the giants of Russian literature; his works include the novels War and Peace and Anna Karenina and novellas such as Hadji Murad and The Death of Ivan Ilyich.

Tolstoy's earliest works, the autobiographical novels Childhood, Boyhood, and Youth (1852–1856), tell of a rich landowner's son and his slow realization of the chasm between himself and his peasants. Though he later rejected them as sentimental, a great deal of Tolstoy's own life is revealed. They retain their relevance as accounts of the universal story of growing up.

Tolstoy served as a second lieutenant in an artillery regiment during the Crimean War, recounted in his Sevastopol Sketches. His experiences in battle helped stir his subsequent pacifism and gave him material for realistic depiction of the horrors of war in his later work.

His fiction consistently attempts to convey realistically the Russian society in which he lived. The Cossacks (1863) describes the Cossack life and people through a story of a Russian aristocrat in love with a Cossack girl. Anna Karenina (1877) tells parallel stories of an adulterous woman trapped by the conventions and falsities of society and of a philosophical landowner (much like Tolstoy), who works alongside the peasants in the fields and seeks to reform their lives. Tolstoy not only drew from his own life experiences but also created characters in his own image, such as Pierre Bezukhov and Prince Andrei in War and Peace, Levin in Anna Karenina and to some extent, Prince Nekhlyudov in Resurrection.

War and Peace is generally thought to be one of the greatest novels ever written, remarkable for its dramatic breadth and unity. Its vast canvas includes 580 characters, many historical with others fictional. The story moves from family life to the headquarters of Napoleon, from the court of Alexander I of Russia to the battlefields of Austerlitz and Borodino. Tolstoy's original idea for the novel was to investigate the causes of the Decembrist revolt, to which it refers only in the last chapters, from which can be deduced that Andrei Bolkonsky's son will become one of the Decembrists. The novel explores Tolstoy's theory of history, and in particular the insignificance of individuals such as Napoleon and Alexander. Somewhat surprisingly, Tolstoy did not consider War and Peace to be a novel (nor did he consider many of the great Russian fictions written at that time to be novels). This view becomes less surprising if one considers that Tolstoy was a novelist of the realist school who considered the novel to be a framework for the examination of social and political issues in nineteenth-century life. War and Peace (which is to Tolstoy really an epic in prose) therefore did not qualify. Tolstoy thought that Anna Karenina was his first true novel.

After Anna Karenina, Tolstoy concentrated on Christian themes, and his later novels such as The Death of Ivan Ilyich (1886) and What Is to Be Done? develop a radical anarcho-pacifist Christian philosophy which led to his excommunication from the Russian Orthodox Church in 1901. For all the praise showered on Anna Karenina and War and Peace, Tolstoy rejected the two works later in his life as something not as true of reality.

In his novel Resurrection, Tolstoy attempts to expose the injustice of man-made laws and the hypocrisy of institutionalized church. Tolstoy also explores and explains the economic philosophy of Georgism, of which he had become a very strong advocate towards the end of his life.

Tolstoy also tried himself in poetry with several soldier songs written during his military service and fairy tales in verse such as Volga-bogatyr and Oaf stylized as national folk songs. They were written between 1871 and 1874 for his Russian Book for Reading, a collection of short stories in four volumes (total of 629 stories in various genres) published along with the New Azbuka textbook and addressed to schoolchildren. Nevertheless, he was skeptical about poetry as a genre. As he famously said, "Writing poetry is like ploughing and dancing at the same time". According to Valentin Bulgakov, he criticised poets, including Alexander Pushkin, for their "false" epithets used "simply to make it rhyme".

Critical appraisal by other authors

Tolstoy's contemporaries paid him lofty tributes. Fyodor Dostoyevsky, who died thirty years before Tolstoy's death, thought him the greatest of all living novelists. Gustave Flaubert, on reading a translation of War and Peace, exclaimed, "What an artist and what a psychologist!" Anton Chekhov, who often visited Tolstoy at his country estate, wrote, "When literature possesses a Tolstoy, it is easy and pleasant to be a writer; even when you know you have achieved nothing yourself and are still achieving nothing, this is not as terrible as it might otherwise be, because Tolstoy achieves for everyone. What he does serves to justify all the hopes and aspirations invested in literature." The 19th-century British poet and critic Matthew Arnold opined that "A novel by Tolstoy is not a work of art but a piece of life."

Later novelists continued to appreciate Tolstoy's art, but sometimes also expressed criticism. Arthur Conan Doyle wrote "I am attracted by his earnestness and by his power of detail, but I am repelled by his looseness of construction and by his unreasonable and impracticable mysticism." Virginia

Woolf declared him "the greatest of all novelists." James Joyce noted that "He is never dull, never stupid, never tired, never pedantic, never theatrical!" Thomas Mann wrote of Tolstoy's seemingly guileless artistry: "Seldom did art work so much like nature." Vladimir Nabokov heaped superlatives upon The Death of Ivan Ilyich and Anna Karenina; he questioned, however, the reputation of War and Peace, and sharply criticized Resurrection and The Kreutzer Sonata.

Religious and political beliefs

After reading Schopenhauer's The World as Will and Representation, Tolstoy gradually became converted to the ascetic morality upheld in that work as the proper spiritual path for the upper classes: "Do you know what this summer has meant for me? Constant raptures over Schopenhauer and a whole series of spiritual delights which I've never experienced before. ... no student has ever studied so much on his course, and learned so much, as I have this summer"

In Chapter VI of A Confession, Tolstoy quoted the final paragraph of Schopenhauer's work. It explained how the nothingness that results from complete denial of self is only a relative nothingness, and is not to be feared. The novelist was struck by the description of Christian, Buddhist, and Hindu ascetic renunciation as being the path to holiness. After reading passages such as the following, which abound in Schopenhauer's ethical chapters, the Russian nobleman chose poverty and formal denial of the will:

But this very necessity of involuntary suffering (by poor people) for eternal salvation is also expressed by that utterance of the Savior (Matthew 19:24): "It is easier for a camel to go through the eye of a needle, than for a rich man to enter into the kingdom of God." Therefore, those who were greatly in earnest about their eternal salvation, chose voluntary poverty when fate had denied this to them and they had been born in wealth. Thus Buddha Sakyamuni was born a prince, but voluntarily took to the mendicant's staff; and Francis of Assisi, the founder of the mendicant orders who, as a youngster at a ball, where the daughters of all the notabilities were sitting together, was asked: "Now Francis, will you not soon make your choice from these beauties?"

and who replied: "I have made a far more beautiful choice!" "Whom?" "La povertà (poverty)": whereupon he abandoned every thing shortly afterwards and wandered through the land as a mendicant.

In 1884, Tolstoy wrote a book called What I Believe, in which he openly confessed his Christian beliefs. He affirmed his belief in Jesus Christ's teachings and was particularly influenced by the Sermon on the Mount, and the injunction to turn the other cheek, which he understood as a "commandment of non-resistance to evil by force" and a doctrine of pacifism and nonviolence. In his work The Kingdom of God Is Within You, he explains that he considered mistaken the Church's doctrine because they had made a "perversion" of Christ's teachings. Tolstoy also received letters from American Quakers who introduced him to the non-violence writings of Quaker Christians such as George Fox, William Penn and Jonathan Dymond. Tolstoy believed being a Christian required him to be a pacifist; the consequences of being a pacifist, and the apparently inevitable waging of war by government, are the reason why he is considered a philosophical anarchist.

Later, various versions of "Tolstoy's Bible" would be published, indicating the passages Tolstoy most relied on, specifically, the reported words of Jesus himself.

Tolstoy believed that a true Christian could find lasting happiness by striving for inner self-perfection through following the Great Commandment of loving one's neighbor and God rather than looking outward to the Church or state for guidance. His belief in nonresistance when faced by conflict is another distinct attribute of his philosophy based on Christ's teachings. By directly influencing Mahatma Gandhi with this idea through his work The Kingdom of God Is Within You (full text of English translation available on Wikisource), Tolstoy's profound influence on the nonviolent resistance movement reverberates to this day. He believed that the aristocracy were a burden on the poor, and that the only solution to how we live together is through anarchism.

He also opposed private property in land ownership and the institution of marriage and valued the ideals of chastity and sexual abstinence (discussed in Father Sergius and his preface to The Kreutzer Sonata), ideals also held by the young Gandhi. Tolstoy's later work derives a passion and verve from the depth of his austere moral views. The sequence of the temptation of Sergius in Father Sergius, for example, is among his later triumphs. Gorky relates how Tolstoy once read this passage before himself and Chekhov and that Tolstoy was moved to tears by the end of the reading. Other later passages of rare power include the personal crises that were faced by the protagonists of The Death of Ivan Ilyich, and of Master and Man, where the main character in the former or the reader in the latter are made aware of the foolishness of the protagonists' lives.

Tolstoy had a profound influence on the development of Christian anarchist thought. The Tolstoyans were a small Christian anarchist group formed by Tolstoy's companion, Vladimir Chertkov (1854–1936), to spread Tolstoy's religious teachings. Philosopher Peter Kropotkin wrote of Tolstoy in the article on anarchism in the 1911 Encyclopædia Britannica:

Without naming himself an anarchist, Leo Tolstoy, like his predecessors in the popular religious movements of the 15th and 16th centuries, Chojecki, Denk and many others, took the anarchist position as regards the state and property rights, deducing his conclusions from the general spirit of the teachings of Jesus and from the necessary dictates of reason. With all the might of his talent, Tolstoy made (especially in The Kingdom of God Is Within You) a powerful criticism of the church, the state and law altogether, and especially of the present property laws. He describes the state as the domination of the wicked ones, supported by brutal force. Robbers, he says, are far less dangerous than a well-organized government. He makes a searching criticism of the prejudices which are current now concerning the benefits conferred upon men by the church, the state, and the existing distribution of property, and from the teachings of Jesus he deduces the rule of non-resistance and the absolute condemnation of all wars. His religious arguments are, however, so well combined with arguments borrowed from a dispassionate observation of the present evils, that the anarchist portions of his works appeal to the religious and the non-religious reader alike.

During the Boxer Rebellion in China, Tolstoy praised the Boxers. He was harshly critical of the atrocities committed by the Russians, Germans, Americans, Japanese, and other western troops. He accused them of engaging in slaughter when he heard about the lootings, rapes, and murders, in what he saw as Christian brutality. Tolstoy also named the two monarchs most responsible for the atrocities; Nicholas II of Russia and Wilhelm II of Germany. Tolstoy, a famous sinophile, also read the works of Chinese thinker and philosopher, Confucius. Tolstoy corresponded with the Chinese intellectual Gu Hongming and recommended that China remain an agrarian nation and warned against reform like what Japan implemented.

The Eight-Nation Alliance intervention in the Boxer Rebellion was denounced by Tolstoy as were the Philippine–American War and the Second Boer War between the British Empire and the two independent Boer republics. The words "terrible for its injustice and cruelty" were used to describe the Czarist intervention in China by Tolstoy. Confucius's works were studied by Tolstoy. The attack on China in the Boxer Rebellion was railed against by Tolstoy. The war against China was criticized by Leonid Andreev and Gorkey. To the Chinese people, an epistle, was written by Tolstoy as part of the criticism of the war by intellectuals in Russia. The activities of Russia in China by Nicholas II were described in an open letter where they were slammed and denounced by Leo Tolstoy in 1902. Tolstoy corresponded with Gu Hongming and they both opposed the Hundred Day's Reform by Kang Youwei and agreed that the reform movement was perilous. Tolstoys' ideology on non violence shaped the anarchist thought of the Society for the Study of Socialism in China. Lao Zi and Confucius's teachings were studied by Tolstoy. Chinese Wisdom was a text written by Tolstoy. The Boxer Rebellion stirred Tolstoy's interest in Chinese philosophy. The Boxer and Boxer wars were denounced by Tolstoy.

In hundreds of essays over the last 20 years of his life, Tolstoy reiterated the anarchist critique of the state and recommended books by Kropotkin and Proudhon to his readers, whilst rejecting anarchism's espousal of violent revolutionary means. In the 1900 essay, "On Anarchy", he wrote; "The Anarchists are right in everything; in the negation of the existing order, and in the assertion that, without Authority, there could not be worse violence than that of Authority under existing conditions. They are mistaken only in thinking that Anarchy can be instituted by a revolution. But it will be instituted only by there being more and more people who do not require the protection of governmental power ... There can be only one permanent revolution—a moral one: the regeneration of the inner man." Despite his misgivings about anarchist violence, Tolstoy took risks to circulate the prohibited publications of anarchist thinkers in Russia, and corrected the proofs of Kropotkin's "Words of a Rebel", illegally published in St Petersburg in 1906.

Tolstoy was enthused by the economic thinking of Henry George, incorporating it approvingly into later works such as Resurrection (1899), the book that played a major factor in his excommunication.

In 1908, Tolstoy wrote A Letter to a Hindu outlining his belief in non-violence as a means for India to gain independence from British colonial rule. In 1909, a copy of the letter was read by Gandhi, who was working as a lawyer in South Africa at the time and just becoming an activist. Tolstoy's letter was significant for Gandhi, who wrote Tolstoy seeking proof that he was the real author, leading to further correspondence between them.

Reading Tolstoy's The Kingdom of God Is Within You also convinced Gandhi to avoid violence and espouse nonviolent resistance, a debt Gandhi acknowledged in his autobiography, calling Tolstoy "the greatest apostle of non-violence that the present age has produced". The correspondence between Tolstoy and Gandhi would only last a year, from October 1909 until Tolstoy's death in November 1910, but led Gandhi to give the name Tolstoy Colony to his second ashram in South Africa. Besides nonviolent resistance, the two men shared a common belief in the merits of vegetarianism, the subject of several of Tolstoy's essays.

Tolstoy also became a major supporter of the Esperanto movement. Tolstoy was impressed by the pacifist beliefs of the Doukhobors and brought their persecution to the attention of the international community, after they burned their weapons in peaceful protest in 1895. He aided the Doukhobors in migrating to Canada. In 1904, during the Russo-Japanese War, Tolstoy condemned the war and wrote to the Japanese Buddhist priest Soyen Shaku in a failed attempt to make a joint pacifist statement.

Towards the end of his life, Tolstoy become more and more occupied with the economic theory and social philosophy of Georgism. He spoke of great admiration of Henry George, stating once that "People do not argue with the teaching of George; they simply do not know it. And it is impossible to do otherwise with his teaching, for he who becomes acquainted with it cannot but agree." He also wrote a preface to George's Social Problems. Tolstoy and George both rejected private property in land (the most important source of income of the passive Russian aristocracy that Tolstoy so heavily criticized) whilst simultaneously both rejecting a centrally planned socialist economy. Some assume that this development in Tolstoy's thinking was a move away from his anarchist views, since Georgism requires a central administration to collect land rent and spend it on infrastructure. However, anarchist versions of Georgism have also been proposed since. Tolstoy's 1899 novel Resurrection explores his thoughts on Georgism in more detail and hints that Tolstoy indeed had such a view. It suggests the possibility of small communities with some form of local governance to manage the collective land rents for common goods; whilst still heavily criticising institutions of the state such as the justice system.

Death

Tolstoy died in 1910, at the age of 82. Just prior to his death, his health had been a concern of his family, who were actively engaged in his care on a daily basis. During his last few days, he had spoken and written about dying. Renouncing his aristocratic lifestyle, he had finally gathered the nerve to separate from his wife, and left home in the middle of winter, in the dead of night. His secretive departure was an apparent attempt to escape unannounced from Sophia's jealous tirades. She was outspokenly opposed to many of his teachings, and in recent years had grown envious of the attention which it seemed to her Tolstoy lavished upon his Tolstoyan "disciples".

Tolstoy died of pneumonia at Astapovo train station, after a day's rail journey south. The station master took Tolstoy to his apartment, and his personal doctors were called to the scene. He was given injections of morphine and camphor.

The police tried to limit access to his funeral procession, but thousands of peasants lined the streets. Still, some were heard to say that, other than knowing that "some nobleman had died", they knew little else about Tolstoy.

According to some sources, Tolstoy spent the last hours of his life preaching love, nonviolence, and Georgism to his fellow passengers on the train. (Source: Wikipedia)

CPSIA information can be obtained
at www.ICGtesting.com
Printed in the USA
BVHW072228110819
555625BV00004B/112/P

9 789389 438901